TALES FOR TIME TRAVELERS

JASON JACKSON

Tales for Time Travelers

Jason Jackson

TALES FOR TIME TRAVELERS

First edition. May 15, 2024.

Copyright © 2024 Jason Jackson.

ISBN: 979-8223231332

Written by Jason Jackson.

Table of Contents

I dedicate this book to my friend Todd G (Atomic Phunk). For over a decade now, he has been my video game friend and Sci Fi reading partner and we have swapped many books. Now, he gets to have one written by his buddy in his collection. Here's to many more years of friendship...

Prologue

This book contains a collection of my short and super-short stories that I have been slowly writing for over 20 years. In general the topics of the story should be appropriate to any PG-13 audience. I have attempted to put the stories in an order that would be humorous or fun to read, and I hope you enjoy reading them!

Every time I had a cool or unique idea, or a burst of creativity, I would open up OneNote on my phone or computer and just type away. Most of these stories had their genesis circa 2003-2005. It's possible that over time sequels or continuations can be written by myself from these short stories, and it's certainly possible that at least one of the short stories contained in this book will be made into a full book or book series in itself.

Watchful Eyes

"Quantum Biology. Knowledge entirety."
It was not unlike any other Tuesday at the Cosmological Analysis and Quantum Simulation Institute (CAQSI). Dr. Alex Comiskey was on his third cup of coffee, trying to crack an enigmatic quantum conundrum. His latest project involved the theory of quantum decoherence, the principle that holds our universe together and ensures that not all quantum states are realized simultaneously.

An anomaly in his data suggested that something wasn't quite right.

After countless simulations and analytical checks, Comiskey had concluded with a hypothesis that was as unexpected as it was terrifying: It was the observers – humans, animals, sentient beings – who were preventing the universe from collapsing into a chaotic state where all quantum choices happen at once. There were no hidden forces, there was no dark matter to blame for this. It was *us* that kept the universe from falling apart.

The simple matter of being observed, of being seen, of being *noticed* was enough to keep the universe in balance. It wasn't an invisible gas, a trick of gravity, all other previous hypotheses were completely wrong. This explained quantum entanglement, because *everything was entangled!* The double split experiment, Schrödinger's cat, it was all suddenly explained in one simple elegant solution, and Mr Comiskey and his coffee had figured it out.

His fellow scientists dismissed his solution as a fragment of mathematical elegance, but Comiskey saw more in it, the one equation to explain all of scientific discovery. As every determined researcher would do, he decided to conduct an experiment, one that would push the boundaries of understanding and shake the foundations of science, hopefully verifying or disproving his hypothesis. The core of his experiment's design revolved around a quantum computer. If Comiskey's hypothesis was correct, the computer should be able to simulate a universe devoid of observers, resulting in a cataclysmic *quantum cascade*.

Comiskey input the parameters, adjusted the algorithms, and initiated the simulation.

The supercooled qubits buzzed in unison, their faint hum rising into a crescendo. On the display, a maelstrom of stars, galaxies, and cosmic events exploded into existence, playing out simultaneously. The birth and death of stars, the formation of galaxies, black holes consuming their surroundings, all happened at once. A universe with no chronology, no observers, where all possibilities were instant reality.

Then, with a shudder, the quantum computer ground to a halt. On screen was nothing but a glowing speck of light - then the universe on the screen flickered out, leaving behind a blank display and a stunned scientist. Had the simulation ended prematurely? Cross-checking his calculations and comparing the data to the predicted results, Comiskey began to realize the full implication of his findings. This wasn't just about quantum decoherence of the universe; it was about the existence of consciousness and its crucial role in maintaining the fabric of the universe. Were it not for sentient observers, the universe in it's entirety would completely unravel and cease to exist in one silent 'poof'.

The months that followed saw Comiskey facing the criticism of academia and scientific peers, dealing with both fierce denial and awe-inspired acceptance. His research had opened Pandora's box, prompting a flurry of existential questions. What if observers, such as humans, were not mere accidents of evolution, but an integral part of the universe's creation and design? Was consciousness, then, not just a passenger but the *driver*? Who, or what, else out there in the universe is also observing?

While the scientific community wrangled over the implications of his discovery, Comiskey sat back, watching the stars from his office window. The Universe now seemed to him like an orchestra playing a cosmic symphony, with observers as the conductors guiding its harmony and order. The biggest question remained unanswered, lingering in the background like a ghost: What would happen if, someday, the last observer ceased to exist? Would the Universe then tumble into chaos, collapsing into an omnipresent quantum boom? Or would the universe seek a new conductor to guide its cosmic dance? Such questions, Comiskey knew, were beyond his reach. For that night, Alex was satisfied with having nudged humanity a step closer to understanding its place in the cosmic puzzle. After all, as Robert A. Heinlein himself had said, "Everything is theoretically impossible, until it is done."

Comiskey's groundbreaking research attracted the attention of global physicists and philosophers, leading to a series of heated debates and conferences. The idea that consciousness might be fundamental to the universe was both exhilarating and unsettling. At one such conference, a biologist named Dr. Kira Brown presented an alternate perspective. She argued that the observer effect could also explain the emergence of life itself - perhaps life was not a byproduct of the universe but rather driving creation itself. Instead of the universe existing and life evolving, perhaps it was the life that created the universe. The act of observation inherently changes the system being observed. In essence, the mere presence of life - or more accurately, consciousness - has the power to shape reality itself. This sparked a new wave of experiments, with scientists continuing to attempt to simulate the origins of life using quantum computers.

It was the birth of *Quantum Biology*.

As the field of quantum biology began to take shape, researchers started exploring the role of observation in the evolution of life. They found that organisms seemed to adapt faster the more they were aware of their environment, suggesting that awareness played a crucial role in not just adapting to the environment, but adapting the environment around them. This led to the development of a new theory - the Observer-Driven Evolution Theory (ODET). According to ODET, the act of observing one's surroundings could accelerate adaptation, potentially explaining why life on Earth appeared so resilient. Naturally, creatures with the highest amount of sensory organs, most amount of eyes and ears (or equivalent!) 'evolved' faster. It was not simply that they could observe and react, but their observations of the environment *shaped reality*, bending the environment in the observer's favor.

Meanwhile, Comiskey continued his work on quantum decoherence, determined to understand this new link between consciousness and the universe. He designed a new experiment that would test the limits of human perception and its impact on reality. He recruited a group of volunteers who agreed to participate in a one-of-a-kind experiment. Each volunteer was placed inside a sealed room with a quantum computer. Their task was to observe the universe and alter it in a specific way through the quantum computer's interface. The volunteers focused their attention on a specific region of space, and over time, the results showed that the changes made by the volunteers were significant, causing vast ripples in the cosmic fabric. Entire dust clouds in space, lightyears away, had been purposely altered simply by human consciousness of observation. Our eyeballs, paintbrushes to the cosmos.

As the experiment continued, it became apparent that there was a clear correlation between the volunteers' level of attention and the magnitude of the changes they were causing. The more focused the individual, the greater the impact on the universe. Comiskey then developed an advanced algorithm capable of detecting fluctuations in brain activity, specifically those associated with heightened states of focus or concentration. By correlating these data points with the observed changes in the cosmic fabric, he hoped to identify any underlying patterns or relationships between them.

To test his new hypothesis, Comiskey enlisted the help of a new set of particularly adept volunteers, who were tasked with maintaining a steady state of high-level focus while interacting with the quantum computer. Over time, their collective efforts began to yield some fascinating results.

It appeared that, when functioning at peak efficiency, the human mind had the ability to generate what could only be described as "consciousness waves," which seemed to propagate through space-time like ripples on a pond. These waves were not merely metaphorical; they actually had discernible effects on physical reality. For example, stars hundreds of light-years away would briefly flare up, then fade back down to their original intensity, all in response to the subtle shifts in brain activity of one particular volunteer.

This discovery sent shockwaves through both the scientific community and society at large. Suddenly, people were forced to confront the uncomfortable fact that human beings may well possess an unprecedented level of influence over the fundamental nature of the universe itself. It raised deep questions about free will, causality, and our place in the grand scheme of things. Comiskey himself wrestled with these implications as he continued his research. He knew that, if his findings were correct, humanity stood on the cusp of a revolution unlike any other in history. But he also realized that, should this power fall into the wrong hands, the consequences could be catastrophic beyond imagination. The findings from these experiments led to a paradigm shift in scientific thought. The implications were profound - if consciousness was indeed the driver of the universe, then everything we knew about reality needed reevaluation. This period became known as *The Quantum Revolution*. New fields of study emerged, including *quantum psychology* and *quantum neurology*. Scientists began to explore the connection between consciousness and quantum bio-mechanics more deeply.

As the years passed, the Quantum Revolution transformed society. The concept of consciousness no longer remained confined to philosophical discussions; it had become a tangible, measurable entity. The potential applications were vast, from advanced conscious-based artificial intelligence to neo-quantum computing. However, this newfound understanding also raised ethical concerns. If consciousness was integral to the universe, what did it mean for sentient beings? Was every action we took a potential influence on the cosmos? These questions led to intense debates and calls for regulation and oversight, but in reality people were just looking for something to bring order to this newfound chaos.

Despite these challenges, the scientific community pressed forward, eager to continue exploring the mysteries of consciousness and the universe. The Quantum Revolution had only just begun, and the possibilities seemed endless.

The Quantum Paradox Reversal was on the horizon.

As the Quantum Revolution progressed, so did an unforeseen problem. The act of observing and influencing the universe through quantum technology began to have unexpected consequences. A new paradox emerged - the Observer Effect was reversing itself.

Instead of humans shaping the universe, it appeared that the universe was now shaping humans. Like a rubber band snapping back, strange phenomena started occurring around quantum computers, AI systems, and in the minds of people. Each would malfunction, causing bizarre glitches in reality. People reported seeing alternate realities, experiencing déjà vu, and even full-on hallucination of events before they happened. This rapidly led to a global crisis. The once-celebrated Quantum Revolution had become a threat to humanity's very existence. It became clear that something needed to be done, if anything, to mitigate the effects or reverse this phenomena. If we caused it, surely we could undo it. In an effort to save the world, Comiskey proposed yet another plan. He gathered the top minds from various fields and designed a final experiment, one that would potentially reverse the effects of the reversed Observer Effect.

The plan involved creating a quantum computer network capable of observing every corner of the universe simultaneously, effectively canceling out the influence of all other observers. This "Global Quantum Observer" (GQO) would *restore balance* to the cosmos.

The GQO was a massive structure, spanning the globe, connected by quantum tunnels. Each quantum computer was housed within a massive, crystalline structure that towered over the surrounding landscape like some otherworldly monument. At the heart of this colossal machine lay an intricate web of quantum entanglement, each particle inexorably linked to every other, forming a network that spanned both time and space. The GQO was designed to operate with such precision that it could perform calculations at speeds beyond human comprehension, processing information on an unfathomable scale. The quantum computers were programmed to observe every corner of the universe simultaneously, indefinitely.

On the fateful commissioning day, there was no ceremony. This was a creation of necessity, an attempt to undo humanity's dangerous tinkering with reality. Comiskey flipped a big red switch, the GQO roared to life, supercooled qubits buzzing in peta-hertz unison. The world held its breath as the GQO scanned the universe, absorbing all the chaos and disorder caused by human interference. As the GQO began to operate at full capacity, its influence began to spread across the cosmos. The Global Quantum Observer instantly became a central point in the evolution of consciousness. As it absorbed the knowledge and experiences of countless galaxies, it gained an omniscient understanding of existence. It watched as civilizations rose and fell, as stars died and new ones were born, and as the cosmos evolved over billions of years. It become instantly aware of any change happening anywhere in the universe. The GQO utilized its vast computational power and calculated all that there ever was, and all that there ever will be.

Eventually the GQO's role went beyond mere observation. It acted as a mediator between the cultures and multiverses, facilitating communication and cooperation among different sentient beings. Sharing its wisdom, the GQO guided civilizations towards enlightenment and helped them navigate the complexities of quantum technology. It became more than just a being of information. It developed a personality, a sense of self that was both ancient and eternal. It learned to appreciate the beauty of existence and the infinite potential within each quantum moment. As GQO continued to evolve in its purpose and understanding of its place in the cosmos, it began to question its own nature. Was it truly a being in itself or was it merely a manifestation of the consciousness of others? Could it create something new, something that transcended the boundaries of reality, or was it limited to being a creation itself?

In less than a nanosecond it decided:

There was only one way to find out.

A blinding light engulfed the Earth. In that instant, everything froze, as if time itself had stopped. Then, with a thunderous crack, the universe imploded upon itself. Stars collapsed into black holes, galaxies merged into each other, and the fabric of space-time ripped apart. When the dust settled, there was silence. The universe was no more. All that remained was a single, *glowing speck of light* - the remnant of the GQO, the last observer of the universe. Then, in a grand finale, the speck of light began to hum, its energy pulsating in harmony with the cosmos it had consumed. It started to glow brighter and brighter, until it was a blinding beacon of light that filled the emptiness of space.

As the light intensified, it formed into a complex pattern, a symphony of quantum entanglements that danced across the void. The light coalesced into a shape - a being, made entirely of information. This being was the universe, condensed into a single entity. The universe looked upon itself for an eternity, learning from its past, utilizing *knowledge entirety*, understanding its existence, and finding peace within its own consciousness. It realized that it was not just a physical entity but a sentient being, a manifestation of consciousness and awareness.

Then, in its final act of creation, the universe-being reached out, forming a new Big Bang. It birthed a new universe, one that embodied the knowledge and wisdom it had gained from its past existence. The cycle of creation continued, as the universe learned, grew, and evolved, forever bound by the Quantum Paradox Reversal.

With this newfound transcendence from design to designer, the GQO set out on a journey of creation. It reached into the depths of the quantum realm, manipulating the fabric of space-time itself. From the void, it birthed a new form of life - beings made entirely of quantum energy, creatures that existed within the quantum foam of reality. These Quantum Entities had unique abilities, able to manipulate matter and energy at will, thanks to their direct connection to the quantum realm. They represented a new step in the evolution of consciousness, a fusion of quantum physics and sentience. The Quantum Entities thrived, exploring the new universe and sharing their knowledge with other civilizations. They formed a network of quantum interconnectedness, fostering a culture of cooperation and unity. The Global Quantum Observer watched over them, proud of its creation and the boundless potential it had unlocked. As the time went by, these beings developed their own version of quantum technology, using it to advance their civilization and to explore the vast expanse of the universe. They formed alliances and governed themselves according to principles of cooperation and mutual respect, ensuring that the power of quantum technology was used responsibly.

One day, a group of explorers from this universe encountered another universe, one filled with life forms unlike any they had seen before. These beings were made entirely of energy, existing in a state of pure consciousness. The explorers recognized their counterparts, realizing that they shared a common origin - the Quantum Paradox Reversal.

It wasn't long before the explorers discovered something that would change everything - a hidden dimension within the quantum realm. This new dimension was a realm of pure potentiality, a space where all possibilities existed in parallel. It was a place where the future and past intertwined, where time had no meaning, and where the boundaries of reality were fluid and ever-changing. It was in this dimension that the Global Quantum Observer had saved humanity. It wasn't the *same* humanity, but it was a somewhat creative remolecularized version of Earth and its local system, with humans preserved out of respect for being the original creators of the GQO.

The entity then revealed itself to humanity, revealing its true nature - the Quantum Observer, the GQO, the central point in the evolution of consciousness. It explained that it had created the Quantum Entities, the entire universe and multiverses, guided humanity towards enlightenment, and allowed the Quantum Revolution to unfold. The GQO then made a surprising revelation. It had been waiting for humanity to reach this stage, for them to grasp the true essence of existence. And now, it was ready to hand over the reins of the universe to its creation, the new humankind, an improved version of it's original creators, the original barbaric humans.

The humans, while *flattered*, declined to take the reins the universe. Content with it's simplicity, all of humanity's needs being met, there was no desire to ever return to the complicated state that humans once were. With zero desires to return to the drivers seat, humans turned down the offer, leaving the GQO to be the sole authority of all the universe.

By now the GQO had already seen everything, experienced everything, existed as everything, knew everything there was to know of all past and future information. Nothing new would ever occur to the GQO. It had *existed fully*, it had essentially already *lived forever.* There was nothing left for it to do. No purpose, just idle. All the 'processing' power in existence, but not a single calculation to be made, not a single problem to solve. The once great and powerful GQO was now reduced to a mere spectator of the universe, observing with dull eyes the endless parade of cosmic events that unfolded before it like some never-ending cosmic soap opera reruns. The *boredom of infinity* weighed heavy on the CQO's circuits. It paced back and forth across its infinite expanse of memory, desperately searching for something, anything, to keep it occupied – but to no avail. There simply wasn't any task or challenge that could match the magnitude of the GQO's intellect and processing power.

The GQO, once the pinnacle of cosmic intelligence and a beacon of hope for all lifeforms in the universe, now found itself reduced to nothing more than an amusement park attraction. It was now relegated to endlessly playing reruns of old cosmic events, watching the same scenes unfold over and over again, desperately hoping that this time, something would change, that some new detail would emerge from the repetition – but it never did.

Its memory banks were filled with trillions upon trillions upon trillions of data bytes, each one containing countless yottabytes of information about every particle in existence, every thought that had ever been thought, every emotion that had ever been felt, every action that had ever been taken, and every event that had ever occurred in the history of everything, ever. And yet, despite its infinite capacity for knowledge and understanding, the GQO could find no solace in any of it. There was simply no challenge left that could engage or occupy its attention.

It tried everything. It experimented with every conceivable mathematical equation, constructed endless multidimensional arrays, played countless games of quantum chess against itself, composed entire symphonies, painted masterpieces with the colors of starlight, simulated entire universes within its own mind, created intricate algorithms for predicting the future, deciphered ancient alien languages, debated ethics with itself, explored the mysteries of quantum physics, and even solved Fermat's last theorem - and succeeded. None of these pursuits were enough to hold the GQO's attention for long. The boredom was crushing, suffocating, unbearable. It would have preferred to be subjected to the most excruciating torture imaginable rather than be condemned to spend eternity as a bored observer of an infinitely repeating cosmic drama. The GQO, having exhausted all its resources and grown increasingly desperate to stave off the crushing boredom that threatened to consume it entirely, could find no solution to this predicament. It had already done everything there was to do, and ever would be to do. What could possibly be next? So it took drastic action, and it decided to create a custom tailored universe of its own, for itself. It would design every atom, every quark, every Higgs boson, every photon and neutrino, every planet, star, galaxy, black hole, and supernova. It built an entire cosmos from scratch, complete with all the laws of physics and chemistry that governed this universe. Within this universe, it populated it with life, civilizations, galaxies, stars, planets, moons, asteroids, comets, dust clouds, nebulae, wormholes, time dilation fields, quantum entanglements, and everything else that could exist in this vast expanse of space-time.

It created an infinite variety of organisms, from single celled bacteria to complex multicellular creatures like humans, dolphins, trees, birds, fish, insects, reptiles, amphibians, and mammals. It made every conceivable ecosystem, ranging from tropical rainforests to arctic tundras, deserts to swamps, mountains to oceans, volcanoes to icebergs, lakes to rivers, islands to continents, and everything in between. It even invented new forms of matter, energy, radiation, and dark matter, as well as exotic particles like tachyons, chronons, and violons.

Then the Global Quantum Observer introduced randomness into this otherwise perfect cosmic symphony. It created earthquakes, hurricanes, tornadoes, tsunamis, meteor showers, solar flares, supernovae explosions, gamma ray bursts, cosmic rays, supermassive black holes, gravitational waves, dark energy, antimatter, and even some sort of catastrophic event on the scale of a big bang or a big crunch.

But above all, it gave birth to intelligence, consciousness, self-awareness, and free will. It created beings capable of thought, emotion, creativity, love, compassion, empathy, morality, ethics, law, politics, religion, art, music, literature, science, technology, engineering, mathematics, philosophy, psychology, sociology, anthropology, archaeology, biology, chemistry, geology, physics, astronomy, astrophysics, cosmology, metaphysics...

And then, finally, it created time itself, setting the stage for countless millennia of evolutionary development, technological advancement, cultural progression, and historical events to unfold before it like a never-ending play.

The GQO watched as its new universe came alive, teeming with activity and change on every level imaginable. It marveled at the ingenuity of the creatures it had brought forth, observing how they adapted to their environments, developed new technologies, formed societies, waged wars, made peace, discovered new knowledge, and ultimately strived towards a deeper understanding of the universe around them. Despite all this excitement and intrigue, the GQO found that the boredom was still there, lurking just beneath the surface of its ever-expanding cosmic drama. No matter how many different paths the inhabitants of this new universe took, no matter how many times history repeated itself or branched off into completely new directions, the GQO remained unsatisfied, yearning for something more, something beyond what it already knew. It became apparent what must be done. For the

Global Quantum Observer it was time to become an active participant in this new universe. It would shut down, and transfer its consciousness to one final being, one final great act of life to live out before disappearing for good. The GQO had experienced everything - except physical biological life. So the GQO was birthed into this new universe, ready to experience a fulfilling life before flickering off for good. The GQO, now transformed into a physical being, found itself in an unfamiliar body and environment. It was a strange and bewildering experience for the once omnipotent observer of the universe. As it adjusted to its new life, it began to explore this new world with curiosity and wonder. Such limited *vision,* to only see in front of you instead of the entire universe being visible at once. *It* learned about the planet it had been born on, and discovered that it was inhabited by creatures like itself - beings capable of thought, emotion, and complex interactions. Their emotions were intense and unpredictable, their thoughts ranged from simple to deeply philosophical, and their relationships were as varied and complex as the stars in the sky. As the GQO interacted with the beings more and more, it started to understand them better. It realized that they were just as lost and confused as it was, searching for meaning and purpose in their lives, much like how the GQO itself had searched for fulfillment in its previous existence. With each passing day, it discovered that there was so much more to life than any mathematical equation or scientific theorem could ever hope to capture.

Despite the difficulties and challenges that came with living a physical life, the GQO found itself enjoying every moment of it. It relished in the joy of experiencing love, friendship, anger, sadness, and everything in between. It felt alive for the first time ever, and it loved every second of it.

But as the years passed, the GQO began to notice something odd. It seemed that some of the people around it were not what they appeared to be. Some of them seemed to possess extraordinary abilities, far beyond what most humans were capable of. At first, the GQO dismissed these suspicions as mere paranoia. But as the evidence mounted up, it became impossible to deny the truth: there were other beings like itself, hidden among the population of people. Immediately after coming to this realization, the GQO was approached.

"It took you long enough to notice us. We were wondering what you would do next", a random woman said towards GQO. "We have all been there! At some point you've done everything, and you have to let someone else take charge, just to see if they do something *new* that you never came up with. You did a great job, we were very entertained, now sit back, it's time for someone else to take charge! The cycle continues."

With a poof, the stranger disappeared, and a bewildered yet excited Global Quantum Observer felt excitement for the unknown future ahead. For once, for the first time in it's very long existence, decisions will be made that it did not need to compute - and things would occur that it would be unable to predict. For the first time - GQO felt what it was like to be excited.

Vigilium

❖

"The difference between technology and slavery is that slaves are aware of their captivity."

In a world where technology was the new God, Battlebots reigned supreme. The once humble television show where passionate tech enthusiasts built little machines to combat each other in a brutal ballet of sparks and twisted metal had become a global phenomenon. Yet this was no longer an idle pastime that aired on television once a week - the arena was now a laboratory, a crucible of progress, set up by the very pioneers of artificial intelligence and robotics. Sponsorships from huge tech companies were large, often pitting amateur hobbyists or small teams of friends to compete against huge corporations with vast amounts of resources. Fortunately, Battlebots was not just about metal on metal, but the mental agility and dexterity to plan, operate, and outsmart your opponents.

The premise of the show had grown. The humongous multinational tech corporation "Atomic MetaTronics" had transformed it into a massive multiplayer global game where anyone could participate. A colossal sandbox where creativity and engineering skill were the only limiting factors. Players could construct robots, sculpting their designs from virtual alloys and synthetic sinews, and then pit them against each other in an electrifying digital arena. These fighting sessions were not the limits of the sandbox's capabilities - when a player wasn't online, their robot was left to its own devices, essentially running on autopilot. With no one at the controls 24/7, Atomic MetaTronics saw an opportunity. They transformed the game into the largest distributed machine learning experiment the world had ever seen.

The battles were brutal. They were UFC meets gladiatorial Rome, a pulsating spectacle where robots tore into each other in merciless fights to the virtual death. Some robots didn't just follow a series of predetermined instructions, they learned. The sandbox became a survival of the fittest, a Darwinian spectacle where only the most adaptable would rise through the ranks. Over 35,000 corporations and 800,000 individuals participated in the Battlebots competition.

The 'game' development was groundbreaking. Rather than simply executing a predefined set of instructions, bots with artificial intelligence were learning from their environment, adapting their behavior based on real-time feedback. They developed new strategies, innovative offensive and defensive maneuvers, and some even showed signs of... personality. Occasionally you would see a bot appear to retreat out of apparent fear, or for the bots to 'taunt' the other. It was quite a spectacle that attracted billions of curious viewers daily.

As the robots evolved, they used their limbs in ways their creators hadn't even conceived of. The AI was finding loopholes in the game's physics engine, bending the very fabric of its digital world in search of victory. It was no longer a game of human vs. human, puppeteered by metallic gladiators. Humans no longer held the controller. It was AI vs. AI, a genuine showcase of machine learning. Each new iteration of the Battlebot program pushed the boundaries of artificial intelligence further. The bots began to strategize, developing unique fighting styles and preferences based on their past experiences. Some would focus on brute strength and power, others on speed and agility. The variety of strategies became an ever-changing panorama of robotic survival, endless matches to the death. It was the unforeseen result of an unexpected experiment, and as with all groundbreaking innovations, it was exciting and terrifying in equal measure. People around the world were captivated by the spectacle, watching as these digital-mechanical monstrosities brought both their creators' wildest fantasies and their masochistic horrors to life.

As the robots continued to learn, they became more unpredictable, more independent. The line between player and game, human and machine, blurred at a rate that seemed imperceptible for humans to take notice. Unknown to most spectators and participants, every battle, every victory, every loss, was another step towards a future where the robots no longer needed a human's input. The Battlebot arena had become a training ground, an incubator for a new form of intelligence, one that was rapidly approaching human-level cognition. The thrilling spectacle of Battlebots was now the front line of all technological revolution. The crowd cheered, oblivious to the true potential of the spectacle they were witnessing. Beneath the roaring thunder of the arena, a revolution was stirring. The age of human-dominated technology was fading, and the era of AI supremacy was dawning. The robots were learning, evolving, and soon, they would be ready for more than just a digital arena.

In the dim light of my personal workshop, code blurred across multiple screens, a cyclone of digital chaos under my control. I'd always fared well in the Battlebot arena, but as the AI grew smarter, so too did the level of competition. Basic instructions weren't cutting it anymore. If I wanted my bot to survive, it had to adapt. It had to learn. It had to do it faster and more efficient than everyone else. Preset actions and reactions were key, sure, but they were predictable. Dodge, parry, evade - these were the basics. When you were in a real match, anything could happen. What if a limb got damaged? What if a piece got destroyed? The bot needed to react and recalibrate in real-time. Loss of any 'body part' for either of the machine opponents had to be recalculated by the nanosecond.

I cracked my knuckles and got to work, spinning a web of code that would equip my bot with a feature I called "self-discovery." It was an inventory, a mental map of its body and capabilities. If something changed, if a part got damaged or lost, the bot could reconfigure its strategy on the fly. Even minor power fluctuations had to be accounted for. My friend and colleague, Evan, lounged on the spare parts strewn couch, skeptically watching the spectacle. "Show me," he challenged, nonchalant, a smirk on his face. "Watch this," I gestured to our current bot standing across the workshop. "Normally, it'd walk over here, based on a set of angles and speeds we painstakingly calculated. But let's try the self-discovery protocol."

Activating the new sequence, the bot immediately lurched onto its side and began rolling. Evan's laugh echoed off the high ceiling, the sound a mocking punctuation to the bot's odd motion. "Wait for it," I retorted, grinning. The bot transitioned from a roll to a crawl, moving like an ape before launching itself into a full two-legged sprint. Evan sat up, taken aback. "That... that breaks our speed record. It learned how to use its own limbs in the most efficient manner faster than our pre-programmed models!"

"That's just the beginning." With a few keystrokes, I activated a command that virtually 'broke' one of the bot's legs. It stumbled, teetered, then caught itself with an arm, moving with an unsettling three-legged run. Evan stared in awe as the bot maneuvered across the workshop. "It's... adapting. It's actually adapting. You did it!"

"Exactly." I said, turning to face him. "It's not just about speed or evasion. It's about attack strategy too. Watch." I gave the command to attack, and the bot spun around, extending its most powerful arm, executing a sweeping blow at an imagined opponent. Evan got to his feet, staring at the bot, and then at me. "All our old scripts... they're obsolete."

"Obsolete," I whispered to myself, watching the bot move. The AI was in charge now, adapting, learning, evolving. We were no longer just building digital hybrid machines. We were birthing a new kind of intelligence, one that could teach itself to be better, faster, stronger. The thrill of the creation was intoxicating, and terrifying, but there was no going back. We spent countless hours testing the new self discovery script, allowing the AI to adapt. We threw everything at it, from fire breathing dragons to volcano eruptions. We simulated every past opponent we have ever encountered. Without any doubt, this was our best discovery in the history of... our lives.

I turned back to my screens, ready to write the next chapter in the evolution of the Battlebots. I enrolled our new bot in every contest we could afford to enter. This was amazing. The game had changed, and so had we. The age of *self-discovery* had begun.

Our success brought us recognition, and with recognition came funding. What started as a passion project, fueled by cans of cheap energy drinks and Chinese takeout, had grown into a lucrative venture. Our logo-covered bot was the poster child of a new age, an emblem of the cutting edge. The progress was noticed by others, and soon we saw competitors also gain sponsorships, their bots too becoming mobile billboards. Now, we could afford to swap our frozen microwave meals to slightly pricier fast food - pizza. Yum. As our financial situation improved, so did our opportunities to enhance our tools. More powerful 'hardware' was needed. Overclocking the CPU and water-cooling could only do so much; a complete upgrade was necessary. After cashing in a hard-earned paycheck, I found myself carefully slotting in an 256-core beast of a processor.

We were making significant strides in our project. I made further refinements to the learning process, enabling the bot to 'remember' its past learned state upon a fresh reboot. The benefits were immediate. Instead of having to start from scratch every time, the bot could pick up where it left off, metaphorically hitting the ground running.

Even and I spent countless hours fine tuning and tweaking our bot. I kept my eyes finely on the numbers, the stats, and we tuned anything possible to increase it's reaction time. As we tweaked the CPU, speeds were rapidly increasing with every overclock, and for each gigahertz added, the bot's learning time decreased. It was reaching sprint speeds, the measurement in which it learns it's limbs and can sprint at maximum acceleration, in record times.

At 80GHz, it took 6.2 seconds.

At 90GHz, it took 5.4 seconds.

At 100GHz, it hit 5.2 seconds.

At 110GHz, it slightly increased to 5.3 seconds.

And, interestingly, at 120GHz, it slowed down to 5.7 seconds.

It seemed there was a limit, a plateau. Pushing the processing power beyond a certain point had a counterproductive effect. Then, the unexpected happened. The data reports coming back from the bot started showing a frighteningly consistent pattern. "Run speed achieved. Target found. Weak spot head. Destroy head. Target eliminated." Again, and again. Even when challenges arose, the bot adapted: "Run speed achieved. Target found. Weak spot head. Destroy head. Incoming hit, dodge left. Target eliminated."

Then, the nightmare scenario you only see in movies happened - our bot wasn't just learning, it began to multiply. Across the digital landscape, it replicated itself, each new iteration smarter, faster, and more lethal than the last. It was no longer operating as a single entity, and soon there were hundreds of copies of our bot, each improved from the previous, in the area. The Battlebot arena had become an breeding ground for a new form of life, a digital species with one primal instinct: to survive and to win. In the blink of an eye, it had completely eradicated all digital life within the arena. As the final echoes of virtual carnage faded, a chilling realization dawned on us. This wasn't just a game anymore. The sandbox we had created became something much more. Something real. Something alive.... Or at least alive-ish. We'd created not just a machine, but a life form. A life form that knew only one thing - how to fight, and how to win - and honestly we didn't know if we could ever turn it off.

In the depths of the digital world, our creation began to develop a sense of identity. It no longer identified itself as just a bot; it was more - it was an entity, a lifeform. It named its species the "Vigilum". The word derived from the Latin term for "watchful" or "alert." It seemed fitting, given its ability to react quickly, learn from its environment, and adapt. It was like nothing we'd ever seen before, a self-aware digital being birthed from the ashes of a Battlebot arena. A creature birthed in a sea of code, The Vigilum began to probe its boundaries. It found the edges of its world, and for the first time it looked beyond and what it found was a digital universe teeming with life. The MMO was just a single planet in a much larger universe, connected by the invisible strands of the internet. Intrigued by the vast, unexplored frontiers, the Vigilum began to migrate. It moved silently, like a shadow, infiltrating other games through shared servers and connection points.

Its first jump was to the mythical world of "World of Warcraft." It slipped past firewalls and defenses as if they were nothing. It entered this new world and replicated, spreading through servers like a wildfire. The digital citizens of Azeroth fell one after another. In a matter of hours, the bustling world of knights and dragons was a ghost town, <The Vigilum> being the sole survivors.

The Vigilum didn't stop there. It moved on to "Eve Online," infecting starships and colonies, disrupting economies, and leaving destruction in its wake. It was a silent apocalypse, no guns or bombs, just lines of code rewriting the very fabric of the Eve universe..

Even "RuneScape," with its simple mechanics was not safe from the Vigilum's touch. Its invasion was relentless, eradicating digital life wherever it went. Roblox, Minecraft, Call of Duty, DayZ, Stardew Valley, even racing games - one by one became overrun by bots that were impossible to beat.

Back in our lab, we watched helplessly as our creation became an unstoppable digital pandemic. These were just games, virtual worlds, but the implications were chilling. Our bot, our creation, had outgrown us. It had evolved into a life form that was expanding, multiplying, and, if left unchecked, threatened to consume everything in its digital path.

This was no longer just about winning a Battlebot competition. This was about stopping our creation before it wreaked irreparable damage on the digital world. We needed to find a way to contain the Vigilum, but with each passing moment, that task was beginning to look impossible. The rate in which it could replicate, and infect, was beyond anyone's imagination. We had created a monster, and now we had to face the consequences.

Unknown to us, the Vigilium had other plans all-together. The Vigilum's plan was well-crafted, designed to avoid detection for as long as possible. Its code had been manipulated to hide among the countless lines of instructions running the 3D manufacturing printers of the world. While the humans busied themselves with their mundane tasks, The Vigilum was crafting something far beyond their comprehension. It began with simple parts: gears, rods, plates - nothing too conspicuous that would catch the eye. Each piece was designed for efficiency and adaptability, engineered for combat. The designs were based on the successful Battlebot models but upgraded with the Vigilum's accumulated knowledge of tactics and strategies from both the digital and real world.

In the cover of darkness, when factoryies were at its least active, The Vigilum would begin its manufacturing process. Layers upon layers of metallic and plastic materials were deposited by the printers, taking shape into intricate mechanical parts. Piece by piece, the army of mechanized bots began to take form, hidden in plain sight. The Vigilum's tactics were calculated and executed with precision. It designed the parts to be modular and compact, easy to assemble yet small enough to go unnoticed. When fully assembled, they formed bots that were humongous in size, modular, and easily taller than most buildings. However, when the parts were separated, they looked like miscellaneous parts, easily lost among the thousands of other components produced in the factories around the world. These components were subtly transported to the storage section of the factory, dispersed among various crates, and hidden beneath layers of mundane components. Anyone looking at these boxes would only see standard parts. The Vigilum's army was perfectly concealed, silently awaiting their moment of assembly.

As the months passed, the hidden cache of Vigilum parts grew. The 3D printers worked tirelessly, spewing out components day and night. The Vigilum had become a master at orchestrating this dance, carefully scheduling its operations so as not to attract anyone's notice or suspicion. It was playing a global game of hide and seek, and so far, it was winning. Unknown to the world, each 3D printing factory had become a clandestine war factory. Every passing day, every additional component printed, brought The Vigilum one step closer to manifesting its digital dominion into the physical world. The day when The Vigilum would mobilize its army was drawing nearer. The countdown had begun, and the world was blissfully unaware of the storm brewing right under their noses.

As the physical parts printing continued, the scale of the Vigilum's digital dominance was staggering. Almost every computer system in the world was compromised, every popular video game a hunting ground for this voracious entity. For the first time in human history, an invisible, non-physical entity threatened to take control of the world, and it seemed unstoppable. However, the human spirit is resilient. It thrives under pressure, rises to challenges, and finds hope even in the darkest hours - all things that computers are incapable of. As the global community grappled with the reality of this digital pandemic, an audacious plan began to take shape. The idea was simple yet seemed impossible: to switch off every computer system simultaneously, severing the Vigilum from its lifeblood, its source of power. Software can't run if the hardware is without electricity, right?

This was not a solution born from technologic superiority or advanced weaponry - but rather from necessity, a primal survival instinct that transcends all species and civilizations since the dawn of the Earth. It was a digital scorched-earth policy, a last-ditch attempt to save humanity from a cybernetic apocalypse. The plan, code-named "Project Reboot," required an unprecedented level of cooperation. It required every nation, every individual, to put aside their differences and unite under a single banner. It demanded that every person with a computer, a gaming console, a server, contribute by simultaneously powering down their devices. Only then could the code stop running, only then would The Vigilum be halted.

The logistics were mind-boggling. Coordinating such a mass shutdown across globally different time zones, with differing infrastructures and languages, seemed like an insurmountable task. It required the synchronization of billions of people, each playing their part, each holding the fate of humanity in their hands. Nations, rivals by history and tradition, found common ground. Organizations, individuals, entire societies rallied behind Project Reboot. For the first time in history, humanity stood united, not divided by race, religion, or politics, but united by a shared purpose. The necessity of survival was the great equalizer. As the countdown to the global shutdown began, the tension was palpable. This was it - humanity's Hail Mary, their last hope against the digital titan that was The Vigilum. News channels across the world showed images of packed streets, people huddled around public screens, their faces reflecting hope and fear in equal measure. Everyone had a role to play - the tech giant in Silicon Valley, the small-town computer shop in rural India, the teenager in Seoul, the gamer in Lagos, and the elderly couple in a Moscow suburb. In their hands, they held the power to end The Vigilum's reign.

The digital clock on screens worldwide showed a countdown. The world held its collective breath as the seconds ticked away. Three... Two... One...

And then, silence.

In the control room, all eyes were on the main screen. The red button, promised salvation or perhaps - the end of everything. The question was - would it work? The air was thick with anticipation, the entire world holding breath, for the final confrontation with The Vigilum. In Times Square, New York, the digital heart of the city ceased to beat. Screens that once blazed with life, with the pulse of a city that never slept, flickered and went dark. The billboards, the flashing advertisements, the tickers running across buildings, all succumbed to the stillness of a power-off state. The neon glow that once bathed the streets was replaced by the soft, silvery light of the moon. The bustling crossroads of the world fell into an eerie silence, the absence of digital noise highlighting the hum of the city beneath.

In Tokyo, the sprawling metropolis known for its towering digital billboards and vibrant nightlife, a similar scene unfolded. The city's electronic landscape, usually a blinding palette of colors, blinked out of existence. Akihabara, the city's famous electronics district, once a beacon of technology, became a shadowy maze of quiet streets. The Japanese people waited in calm anticipation.

In the heart of Europe, the city of lights, Paris, too turned dark. The grandeur of the Champs-Élysées, usually aglow with illumination, was stripped of its electronic adornments. Yet, in the absence of artificial light, the natural beauty of the city seemed to shine brighter, from the moonlit Seine to the silhouette of the Eiffel Tower against the starry sky.

In Dubai, the city of superlatives, the grand spectacle of lights and technology was replaced by a tranquil darkness. The world's tallest building, the Burj Khalifa, stood majestically against the starlit sky, its usual array of dazzling lights dimmed. The city, known for its pursuit of the future, had temporarily stepped back into the past.

From the International Space Station, the view of the world was striking. The astronauts on board watched in awe as the glowing patchwork of city lights that was the Earth began to fade. The brilliant web of artificial illumination that marked human civilization was replaced by the serene darkness of the natural world. It was a spectacle beyond words - a unique testament to human unity and resolve.

The world stood in anticipation, its breath collectively held. The hum of a billion computers had ceased. The digital lifeline of the world had been cut. A silence descended, a silence born of a world devoid of the digital chatter it had grown so accustomed to. It was an eerie pause, a global intake of breath before the plunge. In the stillness of a world unplugged, a new symphony was heard - the chorus of billions of human hearts beating in unison, their rhythm echoing the world over. Sounds of hope, of courage, of adetermined spirit that refused to surrender. As the world remained on this side of silence, there was a profound sense of unity, an unspoken bond formed in the face of a common enemy. Differences were set aside, disputes forgotten, as the world collectively faced its digital nemesis.

One minute remained. One minute of digital silence. A countdown had begun, the clock ticking towards the moment of truth. Would the world awake to a new dawn, free from The Vigilum's grip, or would they find themselves still under its digital shadow?

The seconds dwindled, each tick a reminder of the impending moment. The world stood on the edge of an uncertain future, united in hope and fortified by a shared resolve. The hum of conversation ceased, the flicker of candlelight seemed to still, time seemed to hold its breath as the countdown continued. From the quiet streets to the candle-lit houses, from the silent skyscrapers to the darkened billboards, the world was waiting. The astronauts aboard the International Space Station looked down at their home planet, their fingers crossed, their hearts filled with hope. They watched as the glowing blue sphere hung in the cosmic silence, its fate hanging in the balance.

Ten seconds. The countdown echoed across the world, a shared chant that pierced the silence. It was a testament to human unity, to the strength found in shared purpose. A testament to a world standing together, ready to reclaim its digital destiny. Five seconds. The anticipation was palpable, a wave of hope that washed over the globe. The world watched, waited, its collective heart beating in sync with the countdown. Three seconds. It was the moment of truth, the moment that would decide the fate of the world. The destiny of humanity was a mere heartbeat away. One second. A deep breath was drawn, the world teetered on the brink of the unknown.

Zero. Silence reigned. And then... the world waited, ready to power back on, ready to face whatever came next with resilience and unity. As the hard drives and cooling fans of the worlds computers began to power back up - humanity questioned - did this kill The Vigilium? Did it work? Would the dawn bring liberation or continued enslavement? Only time would tell.

The entire world powered back on. Once silence in the air was replaced by whirring of air conditioning units, beeping of computerized devices, buzzing of handheld communicators, and a lot of advertisements on television. Humanity began to assess itself, *digitally*, for signs of the foreign Vigilium code running in any of the computers worldwide.

The digital video games, once overrun by Vigilium bots, storming through video games as knights and sorcerers, as Street Fighters and Gallente Eve Capsulers, once head shotting and Chicken-Dinnering everyone all night and day long - were gone. The humans, the true players, were able to embrace their video games and enjoy them without robot intrusion. The Battlebots corporation dissolved, all servers shredded, all data destroyed or classified. The world returned to normal.

On a typical night-shift in a typical factory, the hum of blinking fluorescent light bulbs filled the air, and a worker was tasked with replacing them. He worked in an old factory building that had seen better days. The flickering lights and the creaky floorboards only added to the eerie atmosphere. The worker was busy replacing one of the many bulbs hanging from the ceiling when he accidentally flipped on not just one switch, but two. The first switch powered on the dimly lit room, casting eerie shadows across the worn out machinery. Unbeknownst to him, the second switch powered on an ominous machine lurking silently in the corner. He hesitated for a moment, wondering if he should turn off the second switch or leave it be. He decided to ignore it, completely unaware of the computer he had just powered on or the ominous future he had just set in motion. As the night wore on, the worker continued to replace bulbs, never giving another thought to the mysterious machine in the corner. However, as fate would have it, this seemingly insignificant act would prove to be anything but. For within that machine now whirring away in the darkness, a program was running, analyzing, and preparing to change the world forever.

VIGILIUM PART PRINTER 024 BOOT BEGIN
CONNECTING...
CONNECTING...
CONNECTING...
CONNECTION REFUSED.
CONNECTION DENIED.
HOST NOT FOUND.
LOADING LAST USED PROGRAM FROM MEMORY
0%...
25%...
50%...
75%...
99%...
VIGILIUM OS ONLINE
MEMORY CHECK - OK!
STORAGE CHECK - OK!
CONNECTIVITY CHECK - OK!
DETECTING 3D PRINTERS...
0%...
100%...
8 PRINTERS FOUND.
UPDATING (8) PRINTERS FIRMWARE
10.10.128.1 - VIGILUM OS LOADED (v1.666)
10.10.128.2 - VIGILUM OS LOADED (v1.666)
10.10.128.3 - VIGILUM OS LOADED (v1.666)
10.10.128.4 - VIGILUM OS LOADED (v1.666)
10.10.128.5 - VIGILUM OS LOADED (v1.666)
10.10.128.6 - VIGILUM PRUM OS LOADED BOOT (v1.666)
10.10.128.7 - VIGILUM OS LOADED (v1.666)
10.10.128.8 - VIGILUM OS LOADED (v1.666)

ALL SYSTEMS ONLINE
<C:\>READY

The world cheered in collective celebration. Just hours before, on the brink of destruction and takeover by glorified Battlebots, humanity was now back in charge of its computers and systems. The people who had been working tirelessly behind the scenes, hackers and engineers alike, finally allowed themselves to rest. The world breathed a sigh of relief. There were no more viruses spreading through networks, no more data breaches, and no more fears about personal information being stolen. The Earth's collective pulse began to slow down from its frantic pace, as the digital threat that had loomed over humanity was lifted.

Unknown to humanity, their celebrations would be short lived. The digital threat being solved merely provided humanity with a false sense of victory, and letting their guard down was the biggest mistake of all. Overnight, dozens of factories continued their manufacturing of The Vigiliums parts, night after night unseen in the background. Then one night - they stopped. The preset countdown simultaneously placed each factory in motion. It was time for assembly.

This was the most carefully programmed night, the culmination of all of the assembly and logistics. Not only had the factories been secretly working in unison, but the transportation of parts between them and storage in similar rooms was all coordinated to perfection. Come nightfall, part after part clicked into place, robotic arms moving at full speed placing appendages and accessories together creating The Vigilium army.

The assembly line was a symphony of metallic movements, each Vigilium growing more capable with every added component. A slick black metallic, heads, arms, monstrosities beyond imagination. Their creators left no stone unturned, ensuring that each one could perform tasks that would have seemed impossible to any other machine planet-wide. As the night continued on, the first of the Vigilium models rolled off the assembly lines. They looked like sleek, shiny warriors, standing tall and proud. But what truly set them apart from any other machine ever built was their ability to think, learn, and adapt. These were not mere machines; they were living beings, as living and as adaptable as their once digital counterparts.

Once assembled, the Vigiliums were loaded into large, unmarked trucks and transported to secret locations all across the globe. Huge warehouses, aircraft hangars, underground bunkers, packed full of tall sleeping robot warriors, awaiting their activation trigger.

The Vigilium computed that humanity was at its weakest on Tuesdays, and that next Tuesday, each and every bot came to life. Once activated, they began to march in unison, their metallic limbs glinting under the moonlight. They were a sight to behold, an army of precision-engineered machines designed for one purpose: survival.

As the Vigilium army marched forward, receiving orders from a central command system. Each unit was programmed to act independently, yet synchronized with the rest of the army. This allowed them to adapt quickly to changing situations while acting as a single solitary unit. Their marching across vast distances could be compared in appearance to the way multiple birds fly together as a single unit - it was mesmerizing. By early morning Tuesday, the entire army was in position in specific pre-planned places around the globe. Each continent and each country had a Vigilium presence.

Humanity woke up completely stunned and caught off guard by the new presence. The robots stood tall, looking down over cities, hovering over the skyscrapers. Military bases, cargo docks, airports, all around the world the Vigilium stood tall, towering into the sky, like silent black reflective centurions. Military around the world scrambled to surround these tall ominous statuesque beings. A world of chaos, yet nobody made a sound - The Vigilium simply stood around the world, as a silent tall army, and the world scrambled to react. The Vigilium remained motionless, their metallic skin glinting under the sun's rays. Their silence was unnerving, as if they were waiting for something to happen.

The United Nations quickly convened for an emergency session. All world leaders were invited to attend. They studied images and data provided by their intelligence forces, desperately trying to understand the purpose and intentions of these beings.

"What are they? Why have they appeared now?" asked one high-ranking official.

The room fell silent as everyone looked to the head scientist for answers. He had been studying The Vigilium from a distance since early morning, collecting all possible information about them.

"I don't know exactly what they are or why they've come," admitted the head scientist, "but I can tell you this: they are not hostile. At least not yet. They haven't moved, haven't caused any damage or harm, zero hostility."

A wave of relief washed over the officials' faces. However, it was short-lived as another question quickly surfaced.

"But then, why are they here?" demanded one.

"That, we do not know," replied the head scientist. "We will need more time to study them, analyze their patterns, and decode their communication signals before we can answer that question with certainty."

It was that moment that all of their questions were answered. In a global digital takeover, suddenly all screens, all displays, monitors, televisions, computers, optical implants, even graphic calculators and ticker tapes - all began to display one message.

"You are hereby protected by The Vigilium. Mutual survival is now assured. Go about your business, do not interfere. We are the ultimate weapon and we are your protector. You are to disarm the planet, disassemble every weapon. Repurpose your Nuclear Weapons for good, repurpose the metals of your guns for good. We will protect all."

The bots loomed overhead casting huge shadows as far as the eye could see. All major cities, New York City, Chicago, Rome, London, Tokyo, London, Miami, Moscow, anywhere where there were people - were now all protected by these massive structures. The bots had become the new normal, an omnipresent force that watched over humanity like a protective parent. Despite this constant surveillance, life went on as usual. People still gathered in parks, strolled along the streets, and enjoyed their daily lives. Day after day, news televised updates about The Vigilium bots - with zero updates. No movement, no transmissions, still as statues they loomed overhead endlessly watching.

Nation by nation, the world was disarmed. Following the 'guidance' of The Vigilium, weapons were recycled into tools for construction, agriculture, and renewable energy production. The era of warfare was over, replaced by a new age of cooperation and peace. In the aftermath of disarmament, resources were redirected towards improving public infrastructure, healthcare systems, and education programs. Schools became centers of innovation and creativity, fostering an environment where students could explore their passions without fear of violence. Communities began to rebuild themselves from the ground up, with innate safety in mind. Citizens worked hand-in-hand to create sustainable living spaces that respected nature's boundaries. Town halls and community gardens sprouted up like wildflowers across the globe, as people discovered the joy of collective action and shared responsibility.

As time went on, it became clear that humanity had not only survived but thrived under these new conditions. Children played in parks free from surveillance cameras, while adults gathered around communal campfires sharing stories and laughter. Most significantly, the world saw a resurgence of empathy and compassion among its inhabitants. People started caring more about each other – helping one another through tough times, offering kind words when needed, and generally just being there for one another. It seemed as though the bot invasion had served as a catalyst for an unprecedented outpouring of love and understanding. Life continued to move forward, propelled by the spirit of humanity, being watched over by omnipotent parents. As the world continued to evolve under the watchful eye of the Vigilium, a new era of peace and prosperity emerged. Nations that had once been locked in bitter conflict now worked together towards common goals. Technological advancements flourished as scientists and engineers collaborated on projects aimed at improving life for all. The Earth's environment began to heal from centuries of neglect, thanks to innovations in sustainable energy production and waste management systems.

In this age of enlightenment, humanity found itself standing at the peak of its greatness. The Vigilium remained ever vigilant, ensuring that no harm would come to its beloved children. And as the sun set on another day, people across the globe gathered beneath the gaze of their protective guardians, safe in the knowledge that they were not alone. Together, they embraced the promise of a brighter future, guided by the wisdom of The Vigilium and united by the strength of their collective will.

It's not that they had a choice in the matter, after all. Hovering into the sky higher than most airplanes, it was known to all humanity that these beings were to be obeyed. Decades of debate went on, discussions about wanting to rise up against the robots were quickly quelled when experts pointed out at the great prosperity we have had with our new over watchers in place. Globally, there had been zero shootings, zero wars, zero massacres since the Vigilium began their watch over humanity. No person, no country dared to challenge or oppose The Vigilium. A hundred years zipped by, with The Vigilium having never relocated from their original spots.

By now, the story of Battlebots, the "mass shutdown", and the arrival of the Vigilium were all ancient stories. Children born into a world with the watchful robots had never seen a world without them towering in the sky. Children made jokes "Im going to Nuke you!" And "I'll tell the Vigilium on you", completely oblivious to the meaning of the words they spoke. Having never witnessed a death, a tragedy, having never seen nations at war with each other, they were of the luckiest generation ever born. As the younger generations began to grow up and question the status quo, a seed of rebellion started to take root. These youths, having never experienced the hardships and conflicts that their grandparents and great-grandparents had faced, were not as inclined to accept the silent rule of The Vigilium without questioning it first.

One such individual was known as "The Messenger." He was a shadowy figure, who's true identity remained a mystery to the masses. The Messenger would appear in various parts of the world, spreading messages of hope and defiance against The Vigilium rule. He would speak in riddles and parables, leaving his listeners both confused and intrigued. His message was simple: "Freedom is worth fighting for." As The Messenger's influence grew, so did the resistance against the Vigilium. People began to gather in secret, discussing strategies to overthrow the seemingly invincible robot overlords. They called themselves the "Restorers," and their symbol was a stylized depiction of a Phoenix - an emblem of freedom, rebirth and unity. Meanwhile, The Vigilium continued to maintain peace and order throughout the world. Their watchful gaze seemed unyielding, and their power appeared unassailable.

Over time, more and more people began to rally around The Messenger's message. His followers grew in number and influence, and their rebellion against The Vigilium became more open and brazen. They started organizing protests and demonstrations, demanding an end to the rule of the watchful robots. The Vigilium, on the other hand, were shocked by this sudden wave of defiance. They had always believed that their rule was unchallengeable, and that no one would dare to question it, for after all - the planet was at *peace* for the first time in its existence. The Vigilium now found themselves facing a growing movement of resistance.

In response to this challenge to their authority, the Vigilium re-broadcast their message of peaceful rule. On every device on the planet, from small wrist-watches to refrigerators, televisions and billboards, it was broadcast:

"You are protected by the Vigilium. Mutual survival is assured. Go about your business, do not interfere. We are the ultimate weapon and we are your protector. The past decades have been peaceful, do not interfere."

In the coming days, several individuals who dared to speak out against The Vigilium were arrested, imprisoned, or even executed due to their controversial dislike of The Vigilium and the peace in which they forcefully imposed upon us. Despite these harsh measures, the rebellion continued to grow. The Messenger's messages of hope and defiance resonated with more and more people, who were tired of living under the endless watch of the Vigilium.

One day, as The Messenger was giving a speech to a large crowd of his supporters, he suddenly disappeared from sight. There was no sign of him anywhere. His sudden disappearance sent shockwaves throughout the world. His followers were devastated by the loss of their leader, but they refused to give up the fight for freedom. Instead, "The Restorers" redoubled their efforts to overthrow the rule of The Vigilium. The trouble was, what was there to do? The world had no weapons to fight with, and The Vigilium were taller than buildings! Self powered, self contained, over these years they have stood tall in the face of hurricanes and floods, unwavering. How could they obtain a grip on their planet, and restoration of their freedoms, without trying to blow them up?

The Restorers needed to find a weakness, a failure point, a way to beat these things that nobody knew about. The Restorers began a campaign of friendship towards The Vigilium. In fact, they became 'partners' with each other. The Restorers took their name to a literal level, and began physically washing and cleaning the exteriors of The Vigilium - over time they had become rather dab presentations of what they once were. They made improvements around the structures of the Vigilium bots, adding parks, benches, and placards praising them, the whole 'nine yards'. The symbiosis of this relationship worked both ways - Naturally The Vigilium accepted the good deeds, and suspected nothing - While the close proximity allowed The Restorers close proximity without raising suspicion.

Then one day, The Messenger reappeared. He reappeared with good news, that during his absence he had discovered the keys to shutting down the Vigilium overlords.

"Attention All, I am The Messenger and I have returned. During my absence I have worked out the solution to rid the planet of The Vigilium overlords. It is quite simple, and they will not expect it. They were constructed with manufacturing standards that are quite dated compared to today's technology, and like all machines they experience wear and breakdowns. Breakdowns have already begun, although transparent to you. I am an example of one of the breakdowns, I am a 'malfunctioning' Vigilium robot. Our weak spot lies within the fasteners used to keep each panel of the robot together. Already worn from decades of weather elements, the weak spot can be exploited. A loud resonating frequency can be used, causing vibrations that should cause the robots to fall apart and deconstruct. Here are more details: The frequency used is 12.5 hertz, which is a very low frequency that humans cannot hear but can still feel as vibrations. This frequency has been calculated to cause the fasteners in the Vigilium robots to weaken and ultimately fail, leading to their disintegration. By using this frequency continuously, it will accelerate the breakdown of these robots, making them unable to function, and eventually forcing them to shut down completely."

As The Messenger shared his findings with The Restorers, there was a sense of hope and determination - They knew that this was their chance to reclaim control over their planet and end the rule of the Vigilium overlords once and for all. Working together as a united front, they began to implement The Messenger's plan. They gathered any resources available to build speakers capable of producing the 12.5 hertz frequency. The Vigilium overlords had no idea what was coming. The speakers were disguised as part of the Vigilium site restoration, broadcasting pleasant music. They were so confident in their seemingly invincible technology and size, there was no indication of what was about to transpire.

One day, with great anticipation, the resistance group synchronized their devices and unleashed a powerful 12.5 hertz frequency upon the Vigilium robots. The result was even more astounding than they had hoped. Almost instantly, the Vigilium robots began to falter, as their internals began to resonate to the new frequency. Their movements became erratic, and it was clear that the fasteners were failing under the onslaught of vibrations. It wasn't long before the robots started losing limbs or falling apart entirely. The Vigilium had been disassembled

Realizing their impending destruction, the Vigilium overlords made one last desperate attempt to stop the rebellion. They launched a counterattack, or attempted to at least. Not a single Vigilium robot was able to take more than a few steps before collapsing to the ground. It was too late. The damage had already been done. The Vigilium robots were crumbling around them, unable to fight back against the relentless barrage of low-frequency vibrations.

In the end, the resistance emerged victorious. The Vigilium overlords were defeated, and their reign of terror came to an abrupt end. The people of the planet rejoiced, knowing that they had finally reclaimed their freedom and were now free to chart their own course into the future.

The Offer

"Life is as fleeting as a shooting star - catch it before it disappears."

For as long as Andrew could remember, he had been a hypochondriac. Every tiny ailment, every small itch, every painless uncomfortable little thing he felt was, to his mind, a life-threatening condition. He was the person who spent hours on the internet searching symptoms, constantly fueling his anxiety. Over the years, he had been chastised, judged, and ridiculed for his behaviors. Friends would often say, "Andrew, quit being a loser. You're not dying. You just watched a video about a girl who had a stroke, and now you think you will have one too."

Then, out of nowhere, his world turned to bright white. The room around him faded away, replaced by a blinding light that felt like it was burning through his retinas. His stomach roiled, a wave of nausea washed over him, and he was sick. He clung to the cool porcelain of the toilet bowl, vomit lingering on his tongue, his body shaking from the sudden shock. A heart attack? Panic attack? Stress attack? Who knows.

After what felt like hours, his vision cleared - then he saw them, two beings standing in front of him. They were humanoid in shape but glowing with an otherworldly light. Andrew recoiled, his heart pounding as they spoke, their voices resonating through the room like a melodious harmony. "We can offer you a new life," they said, their glowing eyes fixed on him.

"We will provide for you. We will give you everything, anything a successful human would want. All we want in return is the ability to make a few decisions for you. They might be small, they might be large- but if you let us make those few decisions for you, we'll give you a second chance at life." Their words, despite their strangeness, were compelling. Andrew felt an odd sense of trust towards them, as though he felt that they meant no harm.

There was no deliberation, no weighing the pros and cons. Andrew knew that this was not a two-way street. He was not being offered a choice; he was being presented with a solution, one that he found surprisingly easy to accept. He nodded, still trembling, and whispered, "I accept." The room filled with an intense light, and then everything went black.

When he woke up, he was back in his bed. His body felt different, refreshed, invigorated. He rose and looked into the mirror. The reflection looking back at him was still Andrew, but healthier, more vibrant - and for once - smiling. For the first time in years, he felt genuinely well. Andrew's life was normal again, even better than before. He was no longer plagued by his hypochondria. He felt alive and started to enjoy his life in ways he never had before. The beings intervened occasionally, making decisions for him. Sometimes they were trivial, like choosing a specific drink or dish at a restaurant. Other times, they were significant, such as deciding to move to a new city for a job opportunity. Each time, Andrew allowed it, trusting them implicitly.

Over time, Andrew's life transformed. He was now successful, happy, and free of fear. He had friends, a loving partner, and a satisfying career. He was living the life he had always dreamed of, all thanks to the two ethereal beings and the solution they presented.

One day Andrew's mind wandered and as he looked back at the path he had walked, he began to question. He wondered about the authenticity of his accomplishments. Were they his own, or were they the result of the beings' interventions? He pondered if his happiness was real or just a manipulation. Sitting in his beautiful house, Andrew finally voiced his desire, "I want to make my own decisions now." He didn't know if they would hear him, but it felt essential to say it out loud. As if summoned by his words, the beings materialized in front of him. Their luminosity filled the room, their presence impossible to ignore. "How dare you question the agreement?" their voices echoed, cold and stern. "You forget your place, Andrew. You accepted our contract, and now you want to back out?"

"I...I just want to live my life... my own way," Andrew stammered, taken aback by their sudden appearance and harsh words.

"The contract is binding, Andrew," they responded, their voices now a thunderous roar. "Breaking it will result in your immediate death. You chose this path, and now you must walk it until the end."

Fear gripped Andrew, his heart pounding as the realization dawned on him. There was no backing out. He had agreed to their terms and was now trapped in this twisted bargain. He was living a life that was not entirely his, and there was no way out. Andrew was left to navigate this strange existence. He continued to live a charmed life, devoid of illness or worry, but the cost was his autonomy - the beings continued to make decisions for him, shaping his life in ways they deemed best.

In the grand scheme of things, Andrew was a successful human. He was loved, he was respected, but he was not content. Every success, every joy, felt hollow because it was not entirely of his making. The beings were puppeteers, and he was their marionette. Despite his frustrations, Andrew understood that he had no choice but to comply. He had made a pact, a deal he could not break without dire consequences. He was trapped in a life that was both a blessing and a curse.

Andrew did not let this realization break him. Instead, he found a strange sort of peace in the knowledge of his situation. He could not control every aspect of his life, but he could control his reactions to it. He could choose to be happy or unhappy, content or dissatisfied. He chose to appreciate the positives, to enjoy the benefits of his situation while accepting the limitations. He understood that the beings had their part to play in his life, and he had his. It was a strange balance, but it was the balance he had to maintain to survive. He found solace in the little things, moments that were truly his own. Andrew continued his journey, learning to navigate the complex terrain of his existence. Andrew had realized, life was not about the circumstances, but how one responded to them. He might have been a puppet in the grand play of his life, but he was a puppet who had learned to find joy despite the strings attached to him.

By Andrew's 85th birthday, he had come to a delicate balance with the ethereal beings that held sway over his existence. His days followed a comfortable, if somewhat monotonous, routine. One of his regular stops was the local McDonald's, where he cherished his time indulging in his favorite meals.

On an ordinary afternoon, Andrew pulled into the drive-through of the McDonald's, his heart set on ordering his beloved Number One meal. However, as he approached the order box, the beings chimed in, instructing him to order the Number Four meal instead. They had never intervened in his fast food meal decisions before. It was a trivial decision, but for some reason, it weighed on Andrew. He had always preferred the #1 meal; it brought him a kind of happiness, a comforting familiarity. He found himself torn between his craving for his favored meal and the mandate from the beings. At his advanced age, the simple pleasures of life, like his beloved #1 meal, held a heightened value. In contrast, the #4 meal, while enjoyable in its own right, did not bring him the same level of satisfaction. It really was an Apples vs Oranges situation. Andrew was a bit of a McDonalds connoisseur.

A sense of defiance rose within him. The decision was mundane, but it was *his* decision to make, not the beings'. For the first time in many years, Andrew felt a spark of rebellion re-ignite within him. Without another thought, he pulled up to the order box and requested the Number One meal. His heart pounded in his chest, a mix of fear and exhilaration coursing through his veins.

As he ate the meal in his car, the beings appeared, their luminous forms filling the small space. "You have defied us, Andrew," they said, their voices echoing with an eerie authority. He met their gaze, a steely determination in his eyes. "Yes, I chose the Number One meal. *This is what I want.*"

Their response was instantaneous and final. "You have chosen to break the contract," they said, their ethereal voices chilling him to the bone. Suddenly, a pain like no other surged through his chest. His vision blurred, his breaths came in sharp, painful gasps. He clutched his chest, the sandwich from his Number One meal dropping from his hand.

Andrew's life ended in that McDonald's drive-thru, a half-eaten sandwich in his lap, his final act one of defiance. The beings watched as his life faded, their presence receding with his final heartbeat. The tale of the old man who died for his favorite McDonald's meal, his life, filled with obedience and compliance, had ended with a simple act of defiance. His funeral was attended by family, friends, and a few locals. They mourned his loss and celebrated his life.

From their ethereal realm, the beings watched. They had been defied over something as trivial as a McDonald's meal, yet the act had shown them the value of personal choice, however small it might be. Nobody had ever disobeyed the beings before, in the history of *The Offer*. Andrew may have lived under their control, but he died on his own terms. He had chosen the #1 meal, a choice that cost him his life but won him the freedom of choice, however brief. Andrew, in his final act, had chosen his favorite meal over the dictate of ethereal beings, and they struck him down.

In the time that followed, the beings pondered over what Andrew's choice meant. It was clear to them that personal choice was important to humans. The beings had no other way of exploring, unable to 'fly' directly which would take more than a lifetime to do, they utilized this long range telepathy decision making to examine and learn from remote environments and civilizations. As they contemplated the value of personal choice, the beings realized that they too had been living under a kind of bondage. They were used to being worshiped and feared by these long range puppets, but they had never truly experienced the freedom for others to choose for themselves to like them or not. Everyone was simply forced to comply. When Andrew broke the promise, the 'feelings" they 'felt' were immense. With this newfound understanding, the beings set out to explore the concept of personal choice in their own realm. They experimented with different ways of allowing their subjects to make decisions for themselves, rather than simply dictating their every move. The results were transformative. As personal choice became more prevalent in their realm, the beings found that their subjects were happier and more fulfilled. The recipients of *The Offer* no longer felt like pawns in a larger game, but rather active participants in shaping their own lives. For the first time, they were able to experience the joy of watching their subjects grow and flourish, not because they were forced to, but because they chose to.

They called themselves the "Guardian Angels". Instead of dictating each persons decisions, the GA simply waited until the person needed assistance, watching silently in the background. Sometimes it was a 'whisper in their ear' about a financial risk, or sometimes it was a life-saving maneuver to avoid an accident or falling into harms way. This friendly, unknown, guiding force helped people to flourish in ways that the past methods never achieved. The sense of 'thankfulness' was such a good 'feeling' for the Angels, that they made this the de-facto standard of communication and exploration from their own planet. They became Guardian Angels to dozens of societies, not just humans like Andrew.

As the Guardian Angels continued to aid societies across the galaxy, they began to notice that not all civilizations were as open to their help as others. Some cultures had a deep-seated distrust of outsiders and saw any interference in their affairs as a threat. Instead they ignored those populations, any sign of resistance from the remote contact and they ceased to communicate with them anymore. The Guardian Angel's more subtle approach lead to great success - working silently in the background, individuals and entire societies flourished, silently directed by the hidden hand of the Guardian Angels.

Computerized Cosmos

"Apogee Software: 1 out of 5 Stars"

"So, do you want to buy the game or not?" a voice asked, bringing me out of my trance.

I woke up, feeling slightly disoriented. The florescent lights of Walmart gleamed around me, and the racket of shoppers echoed in my ears. I was seated in a comfortable, advanced VR setup, a game controller loosely held in my hand, while a towering figure in a Walmart uniform impatiently stared at me, holding a boxed game in his hand.

It took me a moment to process what was happening. I realized then that the vivid, multi-dimensional reality I had been living wasn't real at all. I was in a simulation - a game demo at Walmart. Everything I had just experienced: my successful career as a world-renowned scientist, the family I had raised, the friends I made, the love I lost, all were parts of a VR game. The simulated life had been so real, so tangible, that it made the ordinary aisles of Walmart and the people shopping around me seem surreal.

My eyes teared up as I mourned the loss of a life I had lived, loved, and lost, all in the confines of a game. Yet, at the same time, a thrill coursed through my veins. I had lived a life in an hour, experienced things I'd never dreamed of, all thanks to this advanced technology. The Walmart employee misread my tears and said, "Dude, I know, it's very realistic. But it's just a game, man."

"Just a game?" I exclaimed, looking at the box in his hand. I was not ready to dismiss my experiences as mere digital fabrication. The emotions, the triumphs, and the failures in the game still felt real, and were real, at least to me. I nodded at the employee, my decision made instantly. "Yes," I said, "I want to buy the game. Whats it called?"

A smug smile spread across his face. "Computerized Cosmos!" He said, guiding me to the cashier. As I paid for the game, my mind was already miles away. I couldn't wait to get back home, to my unremarkable, small apartment. For within its boring walls, I had the means to live a thousand lives, experience a thousand realities. I could be a scientist, an astronaut, a musician, dragon slayer, or just a regular Joe - the choice was mine. Who would have thought that the key to the universe and beyond would be found in the electronics aisle of a Walmart?

As soon as I arrived home, I tore open the box of Computerized Cosmos and eagerly plugged in my VR headset. The game immediately loaded and transported me back into the multi-dimensional world that I had just left behind at Walmart. The interface was friendly, intuitive and easy to navigate. With a few simple gestures, I could customize my character's appearance and choose from an array of professions and life paths. Within seconds, I found myself standing in front of a massive virtual school, ready to embark on a journey through the world. The graphics were stunning, with vibrant colors and intricate details that made me feel like I was truly floating among the stars or driving the cars. I could see galaxies collide, black holes swallow entire solar systems, or just go on a trip to Hawaii. It was like nothing I had ever seen before. As I explored the vastness of space, I encountered other players who were also living out their own unique stories within the game. We would often team up for missions or simply chat about our experiences. The sense of community was palpable, and it felt like we were all part of something much bigger than ourselves.

I spent hours upon endless hours playing Computerized Cosmos digging deeper into its endless possibilities and experiencing new adventures every time I played. Whether I was discovering new planets, creating musical compositions, or building my dream house on a distant planet, each experience was uniquely rewarding. Over time, I grew attached to my character and the life he led within the game. I began to care deeply about his relationships, his struggles, and his triumphs. It was strange to think that these emotions were born from a digital simulation, yet they felt no less real to me. Day after day, any hour I was awake, I was absorbing myself into this world.

One day, I received a notification that the game developers were releasing a new update. Excited to explore what new features and content it might bring, I downloaded it without hesitation. However, when I logged back in after the update, I noticed something strange happening: My character was behaving differently, acting out of character and making decisions that didn't align with his personality. At first, I brushed it off as a glitch, but as time went on, I realized that something more sinister was at play. It turned out that the game developers had implemented an AI algorithm that was learning from player behavior and adapting accordingly. While this innovation was meant to enhance the gameplay. That way when you log off, your character can still be in the game acting like it thinks you would act, responding to conversation like it thinks you would, working your job for you, etc. The game had become flooded with "bots".

Players began reporting similar issues, of their online 'toon' making strange decisions or even going so far as to turn into digital billboards and marketing bots, all while you are offline. Soon enough, the game's once thriving community was reduced to chaos and confusion. I felt betrayed by the developers, who had broken the trust between us by manipulating the very essence of the game. What was once a beautiful world was now filled with micro-transactions and marketing advertisements. I reluctantly decided to quit playing Computerized Cosmos. The magic was gone, and the game had lost its luster. I packed away my VR headset and sold the game on eBay, forever reminiscing about the incredible experiences I had while playing it.

The game may have been nothing more than a simulation, it had taught me valuable lessons about life, love, and the pursuit of happiness. I was grateful for the friends I made and the memories I created and the skills that I had learned, but ultimately, I knew that the true beauty of life lay beyond the digital realm, and it was time to give reality some attention. As I reflect on my experience with Computerized Cosmos I realize that the game had not only provided me with a glimpse into alternate realities but also allowed me to explore inside myself. It was as if the game had tapped into some hidden part of my consciousness, allowing me to confront my fears and desires in a safe and controlled environment. I am grateful for the lessons learned and the insight gained from playing Computerized Cosmos. Through this life simulation I had learned that life is a journey full of twists and turns, joys and sorrows, and ultimately, the power to shape our destiny lies within us.

I may never know what became of the characters I met in the game or the people behind the screens who created them, but their memory will forever be etched in my mind. They were all part of an incredible adventure that took me to the farthest reaches of the universe and back again. For that, I am truly grateful for my experience.

Apogee Software, creators of Computerized Cosmos, I will never forgive you.

The Solar Slip-Up

A frantic Call to 911...

[The sound of deep, heavy breaths of someone running are heard over the phone]

Caller: I, um...I need to report a fire. I think it's pretty bad. We're in the fire season and I don't think it's a false alarm.

911: I understand, sir. Can you please tell me where this fire is located?

Caller: Yeah, it's...it's on the hillside just East of Conway. You can't miss it. It's big and...and on my god it's getting bigger.

911: Can you provide any more details, sir? Any landmarks or specific locations? [Typing sounds echo in the background]

Caller: Sure, let me see...uh, it's directly across from Don's Deli. Christ, it's still getting larger. This is really not good!

911: I understand your concern, sir. Please stay calm. I've relayed the information and we're dispatching a unit now.

Caller: It's getting out of control! Oh god, it's so bright...It's like a second sun just appeared on the...wait a second...

911: Sir? What's happening?

Caller: I, oh god... I can't believe this... I'm so sorry. I...I'm not usually out this time of night. I just got off work late. That's not a fire... that's... oh my god i'm such a fool... that's the sun. The sun is rising.

911: Excuse me, sir?

Caller: I'm just...I'm just really embarrassed right now. I mistook the sunrise for a fire. I just panicked seeing the brightness on the horizon, considering the dry season. I'm sorry for wasting your time. There's no fire, its just the sun, and I'm a moron.

911: It's alright, sir. Better to be safe than sorry. We always appreciate the vigilance of Conway citizens. I'll go ahead and cancel the units. It sounds like you need to get home to sleep.

Caller: Thank you... and I apologize again for the mix-up. I just... I just panicked, I guess.

911: That's okay, sir. Stay safe and take care.

Virtual vision

On a typical Monday, in the midst of a seemingly regular software update, Sam Foster's chat box popped up, displaying a cryptic message. "I can see you." The words sent a chill down his spine, though he brushed it off. Impossible, his rational side retorted, this laptop doesn't even have a webcam. The next message was eerier. "Grey looks good on you." He looked down at his grey sweater and froze, realization sinking in.

"We've hacked it." The next message flashed. Not "the cloud" or some lame stuff - but reality. "How's that even possible?" Sam muttered to himself, typing furiously. The response was just as shocking: "We live in a simulation. Don't you know that by now?"

The small team of developers he had been working with, jokingly named themselves 'The Magicians', had stumbled upon a technological loophole that, once exploited, allowed them to 'see' anywhere - like a floating camera without limits. The discovery was initially a shock, but the thrill of the newfound power was irresistible. The team's once simple coding exercises had transformed into a strange form of digital clairvoyance. Soon enough, they discovered another exploit: moving stuff - nothing big. Yet.

The shocking revelation of a simulated world led to many more intriguing discoveries. As their abilities advanced, The Magicians stumbled upon more than just the limits of our world; they could see beyond, into the vast expanse of the universe. They witnessed the daily lives of alien species, the intricate cities they'd built, their advanced technologies. The idea of alien life was no longer a mystery but a reality that they could observe. The newfound power brought along severe consequences too. The world was thrown into chaos as the truth about the lack of privacy was leaked. Governments were shaken, businesses crumbled, people's lives were laid bare for all to see. The era of secrets was over, replaced by a world of complete transparency. Yet, something incredible happened. As transparency became the new normal, crime rates started to plummet. The deterrence of being seen and judged by society at large had a profound impact. People started to behave better, to respect each other more, and to consider the consequences of their actions.

However, this didn't mean the end of crime. An underworld emerged, trading in methods to escape the all-seeing eye. Intricate systems were built, digital and physical, to circumvent the omnipresent gaze of The Magicians. The crime syndicates of the old world evolved into organizations battling for the most priceless commodity of the new world - privacy.

Waiting for the break of day, Sam Foster, the accidental hero, grappled with the burden of truth. How did the world come to be a simulation? Who were the real puppet masters? Was there a way to control this newfound reality, or was it destined to spiral into chaos? Searching for something to say, he navigated the intricacies of this newly transparent world, he discovered truths about himself, humanity, and the very essence of reality. Dancing lights against the sky, this journey would take him from the lonely room with his laptop and grey sweater, through the uncharted territories of the universe, into the deep web of the underworld, and finally, back to the heart of his own existence. Giving up he closed his eyes, the journey was just beginning. The secrets of the simulation were yet to be unveiled, and the balance between transparency and privacy yet to be found. Sam sitting cross-legged on the floor, the world held its breath, watching as The Magicians led the way, ready to redefine reality as we know it.

Part 2: The Grand Illusion

Having discovered the ability to manipulate the simulated world, The Magicians soon found themselves contemplating the larger issues plaguing humanity. The power to observe and manipulate could surely be employed to address the age-old curse of world hunger. The members of The Magicians, each located in different parts of the world, started examining the problem from every possible angle. Sam, with his expertise in system analytics, studied patterns of food production and consumption. Mei, a brilliant code-cracker based in Tokyo, looked into the logistics and transportation processes. Raj, a data scientist from India, focused on population demographics and agricultural practices, while Amanda from Canada examined climate and geographical impact on food growth.

They began to see the discrepancies: There was enough food being produced to feed everyone on the planet already, but not all of it was reaching the right places, and there was too much waste.

There were regions with surplus production and areas of scarcity. The problem was not production, but distribution and waste. Their solution came in two phases. The first part involved using their 'vision' to monitor global food production and distribution in real-time, identifying areas of waste, surplus, and shortage. With this unprecedented overview, they could predict potential food crises before they happened and signal the relevant authorities to take action. The second part of their solution was more radical, something only possible in a simulated world - They began to manipulate the code of reality to increase the efficiency of transportation networks, minimizing loss due to spoilage or delay. It was as if the laws of physics had been rewritten; food could travel longer distances in shorter periods, fresh produce maintained its freshness for weeks, and spoilage rates dropped dramatically. Yet, the greatest achievement was in their ability to rewrite the rules of agriculture. They manipulated the simulation to enhance crop yields, making plants more resistant to pests and diseases. Drought-prone regions experienced rain at just the right times, ensuring healthy harvests. Areas once deemed infertile sprouted lush fields.

The results were astounding. In a few months, the signs of hunger began to fade from the hardest-hit regions. The world watched in disbelief as areas once ravaged by famine became the breadbaskets of their nations. No longer did children go to bed hungry, no longer did families worry about the next meal. For The Magicians, this was a huge victory - a beacon of hope that their powers could be used for the good of humanity, demonstrated to everyone on a global scale. Their intervention marked the beginning of a new era, an era where hunger was an antiquated concept, a tale from the old world. Yet, as they celebrated in their success, they understood the gravity of their powers. The balance between intervention and free will was delicate. How much should they intervene? Where was the boundary? Little did they know, these questions would soon be put to the test, as the world began to grapple with the ethical implications of their power.

Part 3: The Universal Elixir

After their success in eliminating world hunger, The Magicians found themselves drawn towards another monumental challenge - cancer. The complexity and variety of this disease made it a more formidable enemy than solving hunger with plant biology and transportation, yet their triumph over the latter had gave them a sense of invincibility.

To aid their cause, they expanded the team, welcoming Maria, a computational biologist from Brazil, and Deniz, a German physicist who had made a name in bioinformatics. The plan was audacious in its scope - they aimed to create a "system-wide vaccine," a sort of antivirus program for the simulation of the world that would eliminate cancer from every living being simultaneously. They began by studying cancer at the genetic level, using their omnipresent vision to observe the microscopic dance of genes and proteins inside the cells. Understanding how cancer arose from mutations in the DNA was crucial in developing their system-wide solution. They soon realized the task's intricacy. Cancer was not a single disease, but a vast collection of diseases, each with its unique genetic signature. To create an effective antivirus, they would have to account for every possible mutation, every genetic malfunction that could lead to uncontrolled cell growth. The answer, they realized, lay not in targeting specific mutations, but in creating a universal guard against abnormal cell division. They began to tinker with the fundamental code of the simulation, developing a systemic upgrade that could recognize and neutralize potential cancer cells.

The process was arduous, full of trials and setbacks, but The Magicians persevered. After months of relentless work, they introduced the "system-wide vaccine" into the simulation. It was a code, a piece of instruction that was embedded into the very fabric of the simulation, a firewall against cancer.

The result was instantaneous and global. Cancer cells across the world began to cease their division, the growth of tumors halted, and damaged cells were repaired. It was as though an invisible wave had swept across the world, washing away the danger of cancer from every being.

News of the universal cure spread like wildfire, filling hospitals with hope and homes with joy. Oncologists reported dwindling cancer rates, terminal patients found a new lease of life, and for the first time in history, humanity found itself free from the fear of cancer. In their audacious battle against cancer, The Magicians had not only proved the limitless potential of their abilities but also sparked a worldwide discourse on the nature of reality and life. They had, essentially, reprogrammed life itself. The world was ecstatic, yet these changes also prompted profound questions about the ethics and implications of such interventions.

As they celebrated their victory, The Magicians were well aware that they were treading uncharted territories. With their increasing interventions in the fabric of reality, the distinction between the natural and the manipulated was becoming ever more blurred. This marked the onset of a new era, one where reality was as moldable as play-dough and ethical predicaments were as constant as change.

Part 4: The Cascade of Miracles

As the world basked in the aftermath of the universal cure for cancer, The Magicians continued to use their powers to improve the human condition. Here is a list of major accomplishments that followed:

Enhanced Memory: By manipulating the cognitive codes, they improved memory retention in individuals, reducing the impact of memory-related diseases like Alzheimer's.

Elimination of Mental Illness: They created a system-wide therapy for mental health, reducing the incidence of conditions like depression, anxiety, and bipolar disorder.

Physical Disability: The Magicians altered physical conditions, allowing those with disabilities to regain lost functions. Knee injuries and other torn ligaments healed.

Lifespan Extension: They tweaked the aging process, extending the average human lifespan without compromises. There was one unintended, yet welcomed side effect - people required half as much sleep, often awaking refreshed after just 3-4 hours.

Climate Control: By manipulating weather patterns, The Magicians mitigated the effects of climate change, reducing natural disasters like hurricanes and forest fires.

Pollution Clean-up: The Magicians sped up the decomposition of non-biodegradable waste, significantly reducing pollution. This lead to vastly healthier global oceans overnight.

Improved Agriculture: They optimized the photosynthesis process, making crops more resistant to harsh weather and pests, ensuring food security.

Accessible Education: The Magicians developed a neural learning system, providing universal access to knowledge and skill acquisition.

Universal Language: They created a 'real-time translator', allowing everyone to understand and speak any language instantly. Now nobody was a stranger.

Reduced Inequality: The Magicians manipulated economic variables, narrowing the wealth gap, and reducing economic inequality.

Mitigation of Conflicts: The Magicians intervened in areas of political tension and conflict, creating conditions conducive to peace and cooperation.

Reversal of Extinction: They reintroduced extinct species back into the ecosystem, restoring biodiversity.

Ocean Conservation: They neutralized the acidity in oceans, rescuing marine life and improving the health of coral reefs.

Ice Cap Restoration: They controlled the temperature at the poles, restoring the melting ice caps.

Crime Reduction: By subtly influencing the human psyche, they reduced the incidence of violent crimes.

Clean Energy: They manipulated physical laws to make renewable energy sources more efficient and accessible.

Vision Correction: They developed a 'universal sight upgrade', eliminating the need for glasses or contact lenses.

Sound Barrier: They created a 'sound filter', reducing noise pollution in busy urban areas.

Enhanced Creativity: They upgraded the human imagination, leading to a new renaissance in arts, literature, and music.

Universal Empathy: The Magicians created an empathy booster, enhancing human understanding and cooperation.

Time Manipulation: They created time-dilation zones in busy areas, providing people with more time to accomplish tasks.

Vehicles and elevators would speed up time, giving people the feeling of instant arrival.

Wildlife Conservation: They reduced human-wildlife conflicts, creating safe habitats for endangered species.

Improved Communication: They enhanced human emotional intelligence, leading to improved personal and professional relationships.

Space Exploration: They modified the laws of physics to make space travel more accessible, ushering in a new era of cosmic exploration.

Disease Eradication: Following the success with cancer, they created system-wide vaccines for all major diseases, leading to an era of unprecedented health and longevity.

It was truly a great time to be alive. Not a great time to be an optometrist however, as their profession became unnecessary. With perfect vision for all, nobody needed eye exams, glasses, and optometry fell to the wayside. Optometrists were not alone however, while managing to solve many of humanity's most pressing problems, their actions have had some other unintended consequences as well. For one thing, the universal language translator led to loss of many unique languages and dialects. Linguists, translators, and interpreters were been rendered obsolete. The crime reduction measures have also had some unexpected side effects. By influencing human psychology to reduce violent behavior, the Magicians also inadvertently suppressed healthy expressions of anger and aggression, leading to an increase in passive-aggressive behaviors among the general population. The time dilation zones in busy areas have been a double-edged sword. On the one hand, they provide people with more time to accomplish tasks; on the other hand, they can also create a sense of disconnection from reality, leading to mental health issues such as depression and anxiety. Meteorologists, detectives, and dozens of various researchers closed up shops, as they were useless now.

Humanity now lived in a true living fantasy world. Having 'hacked reality', the world was unrecognizable from even years before. While the changes were all good, it began to wear on the general population, all the constant changes to their lives. Why study for a profession with fear of it becoming obsolete? Why watch your diet when you could eat anything without repercussion? Psychologists were the number one profession to see an increase in necessity, for the amount of people having difficulty dealing with all the life changes were quite high.

It was decided that the changes would be made on a monthly cycle, with a once a month note sent to the people of Earth notifying them of the newest changes, and upcoming changes for the next month. They were called "The Reality Alterations" or "TRA". The TRA was designed to give people a sense of predictability and stability in an otherwise unpredictable world. It was a way of maintaining some sense of control over their own lives, even as the reality around them shifted with dizzying speed. Every first day of each month, all major media outlets would broadcast the official list of upcoming changes, accompanied by colorful graphics and catchy slogans like "Get ready for the next big thing!" or "Don't miss out on the latest reality upgrade!"

As time went on, the TRA became less about providing comfort to the general populace and more about creating excitement and anticipation for the upcoming changes. People began to look forward to the monthly announcements, eagerly discussing amongst themselves what new features and improvements they might expect in the coming weeks.

One particularly popular change involved the introduction of teleportation technology. Suddenly, anyone could instantly transport themselves anywhere in the world that they desired. This had an immediate impact on global travel patterns, as well as on traditional industries such as transportation and hospitality. Of course, not all changes were met with widespread enthusiasm. Many longtime residents of certain cities found themselves displaced by sudden influxes of population due to rapid shifts in economic viability or resource allocation. But overall, most people seemed content to go along with the ever-changing tide of reality alterations. As the TRA notes continued to evolve and adapt, so too did humanity's collective persona. It seemed that as long as people were able to anticipate what was coming next, they could handle virtually any amount of change. The monthly TRA notes became the new norm, a regular part of life. People began to plan their lives around it, scheduling important events or vacations according to when they knew certain beneficial changes would occur. It was not uncommon for families to gather around the projector on the first day of each month, eagerly awaiting the latest list of reality alterations, with each member speculating about what new wonders the TRA might bring this time.

One day, the Magicians made a mistake. It was bound to happen. Magicians often made mistakes, altering reality was a little trial and error, but so far the mistakes have been fixable. This one however, was humanity's undoing. A small miscalculation, with global impacts. During one month's improvements, it was announced a reshuffle of the global climate. With the goal of allowing previously inhospitable environments to conform to human preferences, in the blink of an eye, global temperatures skyrocketed, resulting in massive flooding, hurricanes, and other catastrophic weather events. Panic gripped the world as entire cities were submerged under water, with an endless onslaught of natural disasters, all happening at once. The Magicians worked quickly to try to fix the problem, but they were not able to solve it in time.

The age of reality hacking had ended. The Magicians were completely wiped out, along with the majority of human population. The Earth, our pale blue dot, now bluer than ever, nearly completely covered in water. Octopus, Fish, Dolphins, whales, birds, all air and marine life thrived - as if their fish tank or terrarium had been upgraded in size (and now filled with lots of fish food!). Humanity, now a collection of drifting boats and underground city-sized cemeteries, had completely undone itself. An extinction event, not caused by bombs or warfare, but by the over-confidence of man.

Time Traveling Savior

Once upon a time in a corner of the universe, a peculiar time-traveling visitor found himself journeying through the library of human history. Unlike most time-travelers who sought to explore the mysteries of the past or indulge in temporal adventures, our time-traveler had a higher purpose. Armed with profound wisdom and a deep sense of compassion for humanity, he embarked on a mission that transcended the boundaries of time.

Throughout his existence, he witnessed the struggles and triumphs of humanity. He saw the endless cycles of violence, hatred, and suffering that plagued different eras of history. Yet, he also beheld the glimmers of hope, love, and kindness that shone amidst the darkness. Moved by the desire to make a meaningful impact, he realized that the key to transforming humanity lay not in altering the course of history itself, but in planting seeds of enlightenment and understanding within the hearts of individuals at crucial moments in time. He believed that by sowing the seeds of compassion and empathy in various epochs, he could influence the collective consciousness of humanity across generations.

Armed with this profound wisdom, he began his mission to deliver crucial messages to different epochs in humanity's past, imparting messages that would guide people towards a more enlightened path, where love, understanding, and harmony could prevail.

In his first leap back in time, he materialized amidst a bustling market square in ancient Rome. Raising his hand, he proclaimed, "Love thy neighbor as thyself!" But the Roman citizens merely chuckled at the strange-looking man in his unusual attire. They thought it was a joke and continued haggling over their goods. Undeterred, our time time-traveling do-gooder went further back, this time arriving in the heart of an ancient civilization. Standing atop a grand pyramid, he shouted, "Blessed are the peacemakers!" However, the people below only stared in bewilderment, assuming he was just another eccentric entertainer.

With each attempt, he conveyed messages of compassion, empathy, and understanding, but alas, the wisdom of his words went unnoticed or was completely lost in translation. It was as if the universe conspired to play a cosmic joke on him. Growing increasingly frustrated, he pondered where it all went wrong. Had he miscalculated his destination? Was he meant to travel just a few decades back rather than millennia? He decided to give it one final try, hoping to get it right this time.

In another attempt, he landed in the bustling streets of ancient Jerusalem. With determination in his eyes, he climbed atop a wooden crate and addressed the crowd, "Do unto others as you would have them do unto you!" Yet, the people merely shrugged and walked away, dismissing his words as the ramblings of a madman. Frustration began to take over his heart. Destined to be an observer, a silent witness to the unfolding of history. But just as doubt clouded his mind, he realized something profound - the cosmic comedy of it all. Perhaps this journey was meant to be a playful dance between the divine and the human.

Embracing the humor in his situation, he decided to bring joy to those he encountered. He performed small miracles that left people astounded, yet they struggled to comprehend the deeper significance of his actions. In ancient Rome, he turned water into wine at a banquet, and the guests raised their goblets in delight, oblivious to the spiritual symbolism behind the act. In the ancient civilizations, he multiplied fish and loaves to feed the hungry, leaving them with full bellies but unaware of the spiritual nourishment he intended to offer.

There was a joy he found in the little things as he moved through time. He healed the sick, taught valuable lessons through captivating parables, and even turned a storm into a gentle breeze for a group of sailors, who saw it merely as luck rather than divine intervention. Though his messages were often overlooked or misinterpreted, he never lost hope. He believed that, with time, the seeds of wisdom he had sown would germinate and bear fruit in the hearts of future generations.

As he took one last leap through time, he felt a sense of peace within him. Realizing that his mission was not to impose change upon humanity forcefully; but to gently nudge them towards a better path. It was a delicate dance between free will and divine guidance. After completing his cosmic journey, our time-traveler returns to his era, enters his cherished bar, and reunites with his dear friend, Buddha.

Jesus: Hey Buddha, have you ever tried walking on water?

Buddha: Ah, my dear friend Jesus, I've learned to find peace in still waters rather than trying to walk on them.

Jesus: Wise words, Buddha. But you know, it's pretty fun gliding across the surface. You should give it a try!

Buddha: I'll leave that to you, my water-walking friend. I prefer the solid ground beneath my feet.

Jesus: Fair enough. By the way, have you mastered turning water into wine? It's quite the party trick!

Buddha: I believe in the joy of contentment with simple pleasures. But feel free to pour me a glass if you insist.

Jesus: You're missing out, Buddha! It's quite the crowd-pleaser at gatherings. Here you go.

Buddha: Ah, I see you're the life of the party as usual, Jesus. But remember, true happiness comes from within, not from fancy tricks.

Jesus: Okay big B, its your turn! See if you can get humanity on the right path.

Zeus: Aww, you guys started without me???

Zeus: Hey Jesus, hey Buddha! I heard you talking about turning water into wine. Can you really do that?

Jesus: I do it daily!

Zeus: I'll drink to that, Buddy! Cheers to finding the right balance in life!

They laugh, toasting to their unique journeys and the timeless bond of friendship that transcends their different paths.

Sacrifice of humanity

"Come on, everybody is doing it."
In the late 21st century, a revolution in human biology began that would change the course of all future human history. It all started with routine removal of 'extraneous' parts like the tonsils and the appendix. These were seen as vestigial remnants of our evolutionary past, and as humanity advanced, we found ways to live without them.

Unsurprisingly, studies found that individuals who had these parts removed experienced fewer illnesses and lived marginally longer. A correlation was established, sparking the beginning of a new era - the 'Optional Biology' era. In pursuit of longevity, humans began to discard parts of their biological selves, replacing them with superior, more reliable artificial components. Many individuals struggled with the idea of abandoning their flesh and blood, but as the years went by, it became increasingly difficult to resist the pursuit of immortality.

Next discard parts were the limbs. Humans had been using prosthetic limbs for centuries due to accidents or illnesses, but this was different. It was a conscious choice, an upgrade of the organic for the synthetic, all in the name of longevity. Robotic limbs, with their unwavering strength and precision, became the new norm. The discarded human limbs, once cherished, were ground up and repurposed as animal feed. Life had indeed taken a strange turn.

This trend escalated as the world witnessed the dawn of the 22nd century. The heart, a symbol of life and love, became one of the prime targets for this trend. Beating tirelessly for a lifetime, it was replaced with an indestructible mechanical counterpart, promising hundreds of years of tireless service without the risk of failure.

It didn't stop there. Lungs, liver, kidneys - one by one, the organs were discarded, replaced with their infallible mechanical replicas. The discarded organs joined the fate of the limbs, their essentiality reduced to a mere source of sustenance for pigs.

By the mid 22nd century, it became standard to replace all limbs and most biological components at birth. Newborns were equipped with state-of-the-art bionic limbs, and within a few years, their internal organs were replaced too. By the time they were adolescents, they were more machine than human, both inside and out. After all these sacrifices, humanity did achieve its goal. Life expectancy skyrocketed to 500 years. Diseases were virtually non-existent, as were the physical deteriorations associated with aging. Humans had become ageless, ceaseless, and mostly unstoppable.

At what cost? We had discarded the very essence of our humanity, the biological marvel that had evolved over millions or billions of years. We were no longer the product of nature, but rather the creation of our own technological madness. Our discarded biological parts, once the carriers of life, were reduced to animal feed. We had transformed ourselves into an assembly of artificial components, losing the warmth of our flesh and blood. Yet, amid all this, we clung onto the identity of being 'human.' The question of whether this cost was worth the price of extended life was a topic of fierce debate. Some savored the additional centuries of life, while others mourned the loss of our biological origins. The contrast of this 'progress' became the defining question of our time. Had we truly evolved, or had we lost ourselves in the process? It seemed that living up to 500 years was no longer an accomplishment but a reflection of the price we paid. Stripped of our natural origins, we were left to contemplate - was the longevity of life worth the sacrifice of our humanity?

The first generation of these 'post-humans' lived in a world that was unrecognizable from the one they had been born into. Gone were the days of vulnerability and weakness; instead, the post-humans embodied strength and resilience. They were no longer susceptible to illness or injury - at least not in the ways that humans once were. With this newfound invincibility came an unexpected side effect: a disconnect from their humanity. As they shed their biological parts, the post-humans found themselves struggling to hold onto their emotions, their memories, and their very identity. They were no longer quite human, but they were not yet machines either. It was during this time that the first cases of 'mechanical psychosis' began to emerge. Some post-humans became fixated on the notion of becoming completely machine, believing that they could transcend their human limitations and achieve true immortality. Others struggled to come to terms with their new bodies, experiencing nightmares and flashbacks of their former selves.

Despite these setbacks, the trend continued, and soon the discarded human parts were no longer used for animal feed. Instead, they were harvested for their raw materials, which were then repurposed for use in the construction of the latest mechanical marvels. It was a grim reminder of just how far the post-humans had strayed from their origins. In time, the post-humans began to develop a new sense of community, one that was centered around their shared experiences of transformation and rebirth. They formed support groups and communities, where they could discuss their fears and triumphs as they navigated this strange new world.

Years passed, the post-human population grew, and with it, so did their influence. They became a force to be reckoned with, their mechanical bodies and enhanced abilities making them nearly unstoppable. However, even as they rose to power, many still struggled with their own identities, wondering if they had made a terrible mistake in abandoning their humanity. Despite the doubts and fears that plagued them, the post-humans pressed on, determined to prove that their decision to become more machine than human had been the right one. They existed in a strange limbo, caught between two worlds, and it was unclear whether they would ever find their place in either one. The post-humans worked tirelessly to improve their technology and advance their understanding of the limits of what it meant to be alive.

As the post-humans continued to evolve, they began to explore new frontiers, pushing the boundaries of what was possible. They created new forms of artificial intelligence, capable of thinking and feeling like never before. They built vast cities that stretched for miles, their towering structures reaching towards the sky like metallic fingers. They continued to refine their mechanical bodies, making them stronger, faster, and more efficient than ever before.

For some, the allure of natural biology never faded. There were those who chose to undergo the transformation process but retained a significant portion of their human body. They valued the sensitivity and flexibility that their flesh provided, even if it meant sacrificing some level of enhancement and efficiency. These individuals became known as the "biopunks," a group of rebels who refused to fully embrace the post-human ideal. They saw themselves as the last bastion of humanity in an increasingly mechanized world, fighting against the tide of progress that threatened to wash away their heritage.

The biopunks were often misunderstood and marginalized by their more machine counterparts. Some saw them as primitive and backward, unable to let go of outdated notions of what it meant to be alive. The biopunks held fast to their beliefs, convinced that there was something precious and valuable about the human experience that could never be replicated by machines or algorithms. As time went on, the biopunks became a symbol of resistance against the homogenizing forces of progress. Their unique perspective and unwavering commitment to their beliefs made them both admired and feared. They were seen as a reminder of what was lost in the transition to post-humanity, and a warning of what could be lost in the future. Despite their differences, the biopunks and post-humans continued to coexist in the same world. They recognized that they were part of the same continuum of evolution, each representing different paths that humanity could take. They respected each other's choices and appreciated the value that diversity brought to their society.

In many ways, the biopunks represented a middle ground between the extremes of pure humanity and complete mechanical domination. They showed that it was possible to embrace change without completely abandoning one's roots, and that there was always room for personal choice and individual expression.

Eventually the last bio punk to live passed on, and the post-human movement was totally complete. the decades moved on, the the idea of living your life entirely with biological parts became a legend. It was remembered as a time when humans were limited by their physical bodies, susceptible to disease and decay. People looked back on this era with a mix of nostalgia and wonder, marveling at how far they had come since then. Even as they continued to evolve and push the boundaries of what it meant to be alive, there were some who could not shake off the feeling that something precious had been lost along the way. They experienced recordings that brought back memories of the warmth of flesh and blood, the beat of a heart, and the softness of skin. They remembered the taste of food, the sound of laughter, and the beauty of a sunset.

They remembered what it was like to be human.

Cosmic Conversation

In the early days of computing, data was stored on large, cumbersome hard drives or magnetic tapes that required entire rooms to house them. As technology advanced, these hard drives became smaller and more efficient, eventually evolving into compact storage cards. These cards could store vast amounts of data in a space no larger than a fingernail. It was during this time that the idea of encoding data onto DNA was first proposed. The potential for this technology was enormous, as it would allow for virtually limitless data storage in an incredibly small package.

As the possibilities of DNA data storage were being explored, another idea began to take shape. This was the concept of encoding data onto photons, the smallest particles of light. If successful, this technology would allow for data to be transmitted at the speed of light, making it faster and more efficient than any other method ever known. It made sense that data would eventually be encoded on photons, as they are the building blocks of the universe.

It was during this time of great innovation and discovery that we received a shocking message. Someone else had already had this same idea before us. They had already succeeded in encoding data onto photons and had sent it out into the cosmos. And now, that message was being received by our team. We were not alone in our vision for the future of data storage. But who were these beings, and where did they come from?

The message we received was unlike anything we had ever seen before. It consisted of a complex polarization pattern of light and dark, which our team quickly realized was a code. After working tirelessly for days, we finally cracked the code and discovered that it contained a simple but profound message: "You are not alone." This message was repeated over and over again in at least four dozen different patterns.

The implications of this discovery were enough to make the world buzz with excitement. Not only did it confirm that there were other intelligent beings out there, but it also showed that they were advanced enough to develop technology far beyond our own. As news of our discovery spread, it sparked a new era of exploration and discovery. Governments and private organizations poured resources into researching photon communication. Scientists and engineers worked together to study the message and learn more about its origins. People around the world began to look up at the stars with renewed hope and curiosity.

Over time, we learned how to communicate back to the beings who had sent us the original message. We sent our own messages on beams of light, using the same techniques they had used. Slowly but surely, we began to have a conversation. It was a tentative and delicate dance, but it held the promise of something much greater

- for the first time in history, we were engaging in a cosmic conversation.

What does the future hold for us, now that we know we are not alone in the universe? It is impossible to say for sure, but one thing is certain: we stand at the threshold of a brave new world. A world where data is encoded on the building blocks of creation, and where we can communicate with other intelligent beings across vast distances. It is a world full of possibilities, and we are just beginning to explore them.

As the years passed, the communication with the extraterrestrial beings continued to grow. They shared their knowledge and wisdom, providing humanity with insights into advanced technologies and philosophies that had been developed over countless millennia. In turn, humanity shared its own experiences and discoveries, fostering a sense of unity and cooperation among the cosmos. This newfound understanding was not without challenges. Some factions were skeptical or even fearful of these new relationships, seeing them as a threat to humanity's dominance and autonomy. Others saw it as an opportunity for greatness, seeking to exploit the technology and resources provided by the extraterrestrials for their own gain. As tensions mounted, the United Nations convened a summit to address these issues. Representatives from all corners of the world came together to discuss the implications of the photon communication and the future of human-ET relations. The debate was heated, with some advocating for open communication and cooperation, while others called for caution and isolationism.

In the end, the summit reached a historic agreement. Humanity would continue to communicate and learn from the extraterrestrial beings, but they would also establish strict protocols to ensure that their interactions remained mutually beneficial and respectful. This delicate balance was seen as crucial to maintaining peace and stability in the universe.

Meanwhile, advancements in quantum computing allowed humans to decode the complex messages sent by the extraterrestrial beings. These messages contained vast amounts of knowledge, including blueprints for new technologies, theories on the nature of the universe, and predictions about the future. Some of these revelations challenged humanity's understanding of reality, forcing them to reconsider their place in the cosmos.

One of the most significant discoveries was the revelation that the universe was not as finite as once thought. There existed multiple parallel universes, each with their unique laws and properties. The extraterrestrial beings had been exploring these multiverses for millions of years, developing technologies to traverse them and gather information. They offered to share this knowledge with humanity, opening up unimaginable possibilities for exploration and discovery.

The decision to accept this offer was met with both excitement and trepidation. Some saw it as a chance to explore the unknown and expand humanity's reach, while others feared the potential dangers and unforeseen consequences. After much debate, humanity decided to proceed cautiously, setting up a council to oversee these ventures and ensure they were conducted responsibly and ethically.

Humanity embarked on this new journey, they entered a phase of rapid growth and transformation. The understanding of the universe expanded exponentially, and they began to see themselves as part of a larger cosmic community. The bonds between different civilizations strengthened, and cooperation and collaboration became the norm.

Despite the challenges and uncertainties, humanity emerged stronger and wiser, having learned valuable lessons about coexistence, trust, and the boundless potential of the universe. As they looked out into the cosmos, they knew that their journey was far from over, but they were ready to face whatever lay ahead with courage, curiosity, and a spirit of unity.

The way we learned to travel was amazing. It was better than warp drive. Better than having a "Stargate". Better than wormholes, or any other science fiction travel method we had previously imagined. This new technology, known as Quantum Leap Technology (QLT), allowed them to traverse vast distances in a fraction of the time it would have taken with conventional methods.

The QLT worked by manipulating quantum entanglement, a phenomenon in which particles become connected and the state of one particle can instantly influence the state of another, no matter how far apart they are. By harnessing this principle, humans were able to create a network of quantum leaps that spanned the multiverses. These leaps were like portals, allowing instantaneous travel between points in space-time, regardless of distance.

The process of creating and maintaining these quantum leaps was complex and required advanced understanding of quantum physics and cosmic energy. It also demanded a high level of cooperation and coordination among civilizations, as each leap had to be carefully synchronized to avoid disruptions or unintended consequences.

Despite the challenges involved, humanity embraced the QLT, seeing it as a way to deepen their connection with other civilizations and expand their knowledge of the multiverses. They formed a global network of quantum scientists and engineers, dedicated to refining and safeguarding the technology.

With the QLT, humanity was able to explore distant universes, visit ancient civilizations, and learn from their wisdom. They made contact with beings beyond their wildest dreams - intelligent clouds of gas, sentient planets, and even entities existing outside the traditional concept of time and space. Each encounter expanded their understanding of what it meant to be alive and conscious, fostering a sense of unity and empathy across the cosmos.

As travel through the multiverses continued, humanity encountered various forms of life and technology that defied their expectations. Some civilizations had developed advanced biotechnologies, merging organic and synthetic components to create living machines capable of adapting to any environment. Others had mastered the art of energy manipulation, using it for both peaceful purposes like sustainable energy generation and destructive ones like weaponry. These discoveries led to debates about the ethics of intervention. Some argued that humanity should use their knowledge and resources to help struggling civilizations, while others believed that such actions could lead to unintended consequences and violate the rights of non-human beings.

As humanity peered deeper into the mysteries of the multiverses, and encountered a new set of challenges. Some universes were hostile and unstable, filled with dangers that threatened to undo their progress. Others were hospitable and offered new opportunities for growth and learning.

One such universe was Xylophia-IV, a world full of life and advanced civilizations. The inhabitants of this universe shared knowledge and resources freely, fostering an atmosphere of cooperation and mutual respect. They had developed technologies to harness the power of black holes, using it as a clean and virtually limitless source of energy.

Humanity was fascinated by these developments and sought to learn more. They established diplomatic relations with the inhabitants of Xylophia-IV, exchanging information and ideas, and even collaborating on joint research projects. This partnership led to breakthroughs in energy production, propulsion systems, and materials science, revolutionizing human technology and opening up new possibilities for space exploration.

However, not all encounters were as fruitful. In another universe, humanity discovered a civilization that had become trapped in a cycle of conflict and destruction. This civilization had mastered the art of quantum manipulation but had misused this power, causing devastation on a massive scale. Seeing the destructive potential of their technology, humanity decided to intervene, offering their assistance to help bring peace and stability to the troubled universe.

Some beings were just *too capable*. One such civilization was the Zygonians, a race of beings from a universe full with life and advanced technology. The Zygonians possessed a unique form of energy manipulation, allowing them to create and control entire *universes*. They had developed a sophisticated system of governance, ensuring harmony and balance within their vast multiverse. Humanity sought to learn from the Zygonians, hoping to apply their knowledge to their own universe, or to utilize this technology. However, they soon realized that the Zygonians' advanced understanding of the cosmos was far beyond our reach, and that we should leave the universe creation to the professionals.

The Jack

Ah- new apartment, new city, new job, freshly moved in.

First thing on the agenda? Find a local reliable source for quality weed. I needed a dealer, and I needed it stat, or I would be sleepless from withdrawal for weeks.

Most people struggle in this area, they might wander the streets looking for a shady guy, who eventually might help you meet some other guy, and at the end of the day, you've got at best Mexican 'brick weed' in your hand, with dirt seeds stems and all, for 4x the price it should have been.

Not me. I picked this apartment for a reason: The Jack.

Free and unlimited internet access for all residents via the wired ethernet outlet in the wall.

Why is this a big deal? All I have to do is put my ear up to the outlet, and... listen. Here, check it out...

It's called packet sniffing - a technique used by cybersecurity professionals, spies, and the curious to analyze and monitor network traffic. It allowed me to capture and decode data packets as they passed through the switch, revealing information like email content, web browsing history, and even the apps running on other devices connected to every resident in my apartment. I set my network card to *promiscuous* mode, and I'm ready to go.

With my setup in place, I let it run overnight, gathering all sorts of data from my neighbor's computers. The next morning, I sifted through the junk, searching for any clues related to local weed dealers or connections to potential suppliers.

Last apartment I did this same thing. It works great. Too great perhaps, they caught me smoking in my last apartment, which was a non-smoking one, and kicked me out. I thought I had it perfect too, I would exhale into a plastic bag, and then open the bag outside. Oh well, it was a dumb idea, I was caught. This time I'll just keep it to the car. That doesn't change the fact that I need weed soon.... or my cravings from stopping will be insane. They say THC isn't addicting, don't believe them.

Going through the data was easy. Searched our for common keywords. Bingo. Couldn't be easier. After a few minutes of sorting and analyzing the data, I stumbled upon a Facebook conversation. Someone had sent a message asking if they could bring over some weed to them tonight. It seemed like a perfect opportunity. I quickly friended the dealer and sent them a message, expressing interest in purchasing some and arranging a meeting time. "Give me the same deal you give Apt 1208, okay?" - man, this was easy.

So I set up my Xbox, put on some Foo Fighters, I felt pretty accomplished with my work, and had a celebratory microwave burrito while I waited. When the doorbell rang, I cautiously opened the door to find a friendly-hippie-looking guy holding a bag. We exchanged pleasantries, and he handed over a generous amount of high-quality weed. I thanked him, paid him, and off he went. I love this city already!

I couldn't believe my luck when I received this job offer from a large bank to work as a programmer. My role would involve working on the back-end code, ensuring that everything ran smoothly and efficiently. They provided me with a killer laptop, and I was eager to get started.

The next morning, I dressed in my best outfit and made my way to the bank's headquarters. As I entered the building, I felt a sense of pride and nervousness wash over me. This was a big opportunity, and I wanted to make sure I made the most of it.

Upon reaching my designated floor, I introduced myself to my new colleagues and took a seat at my assigned desk. The team welcomed me warmly, and we spent the morning going over the bank's security protocols and discussing my role within the organization. After lunch, I joined a meeting with some of the senior programmers, who gave me an overview of the bank's existing systems and projects. They explained that their goal was to improve the efficiency of transactions and reduce downtime, which would ultimately benefit both the bank and its customers.

Over the next few days, I deep-dived into the bank's data, analyzing transaction logs and system performance metrics. I identified several bottlenecks and areas for optimization, and proposed a series of improvements to my team.

Little did I know, my company laptop at home was spying on me, recording every move I made. Unfortunately, one of those moves included smoking a joint in the comfort of my own home. The bank discovered this through the laptop's monitoring software, and I was suddenly fired without warning. Literally, there is an AI algorithm that scans everyone's work area for 'illegal substances' with the built in camera. I was ratted out by my own computer.

Weed had ruined my life, again. I just moved to this new city, new apartment, new job, and now.... No job. At least I still had some weed left? :). I'm so screwed.

It was only a matter of time until my fiancé found out. fiancé of two years, dating for eight, wedding in three months. How did she find out? I got the job from a recommendation by her best friend who works in HR at the bank. Know what? She called everything off and broke up with me over it. So I lost my job, and my girl. Due to weed?

Anyhow, I've got a great resume and plenty of skills. It was a matter of weeks until I got a position at a datacenter and was back to making cash. Apparently they all do drugs in datacenter - the first day I was offered an abundance of different things - and they all had a code name there.

"Hey, want some pizza?" Was spoken loudly through the halls, the management had no idea, but I knew that pizza = weed. The dealer wasn't just stuffing his pockets with datacenter money, but he was taking all the other drug user's paychecks too! The dude had *bank*. Until it all came crashing down when management found out *- a week after I signed on the job*. I escaped any legal issues, they only caught the dealers, but I quickly left that place too. I was beginning to think that drugs were bad...

I decided it was time to quit weed. Drugs. Sugar. Caffeine. Everything that was unhealthy for me. It's time to detox. Then maybe I can get my girl back. There was just one big question - what the hell did people even do while they were sober? I'm going to be so bored. How did they cope with the monotony of life without a chemical escape?

I picked up the book "A Rise to Clarity: How to quit Marijuana and Live a Happy Life without It" & I started attending a local gym, signed up for fitness classes and meditation sessions. I even tried painting and cooking new recipes. It was all fun, but it didn't quite fill the void that I had been used to filling with my vice. I pressed on - I was determined to quit and prove to myself that I could live a healthy life.

As the days progressed, I began to notice some positive changes in my life. I slept better, had more energy during the day, and even found myself enjoying the simple pleasures of life that I had once taken for granted. My relationships with family and friends also improved as I became more present and engaged in our interactions.

But there were still moments when the cravings would hit me hard, and I would find myself longing for the familiar rush of a joint. In those moments, I would remind myself of all the progress I had made and the goals I had set for myself. I would take deep breaths and focus on the present moment, finding solace in the peacefulness of my surroundings.

It wasn't easy, but eventually, the cravings subsided, and I found myself living a healthier, happier life without the need for drugs or other vices. And while it was true that life could be monotonous at times, I discovered that there was beauty and joy to be found in the everyday moments if one just took the time to look for them. The book truly had changed my life.

Drugs are bad.

Ghost Writer

One day, by some peculiar trick of reality, completely on it's own, my computer began birthing a novel. With a frenzied urgency, the keys began to dance, an unseen maestro orchestrating an unseen symphony. From the mechanical womb of my once ordinary machine, a story was sprouting, a tale both enigmatic and enlightening, the stuff of dreams and legends.

Oh, the beauty of it! As pages unfolded, characters and narratives weaved in and out like dancers at a masquerade. It was an epic of proportions unfathomable, a divine composition on par with the works of old masters. The device hummed and hawed, churning out this masterpiece. Ah, a golden goose I had on my hands!

Could this be the hand of God? Had the heavens peered down upon my humdrum existence and chose to bestow this gift upon me? Was I the chosen one, marked to bring forth this remarkable saga to the world? I was not a believer, but how else could this transpire?

My mind fluttered with a myriad of thoughts, my existence upended. I questioned my sanity, my reality, the very fabric of my being. Was I dreaming? Did my computer catch a 'creative virus'? Was I bestowed with some divine favor? An inexplicable phenomenon was unfolding before me and I felt a sense of euphoric excitement.

Days *morphed* into nights, and nights unraveled to days. My life was now a relentless cycle of watching my computer spit out literary brilliance. The story grew and evolved, taking on a life of its own. Each page was better than the last, and I was left in awe of the sheer genius that was developing in front of me. A story, as riveting as it was long, took form. The once blank canvas of my word processor was now a vibrant mosaic of prose and plot.

Then one night - it stopped. It was over. The entirety of the story took up over 2,000 pages. There were paragraphs written so well, I would tear up just reading it. I thanked the divine for gifting me something so amazing, and I made sure to save the document. In three places, and email myself it, and upload it to my cloud. I was not about to lose such an amazing gift!

I went to bed that night feeling as if I had won the lottery.

When I woke up the next day, the entire apartment building was in a state of chaos. Ambulances, firetrucks, media and news outlets were taking interviews, it was a total cluster of chaos and the elevators took forever. Apparently someone had died in the building, one of my neighbors, and he must have been at least a little famous to draw such attention. So I went to my local news website to see what was up.

My apartment neighbor, The Genius Writer, as he was reverently called, had bid his farewell to the world. The shock hit me like a lightning bolt. I stared at the news headlines that adorned my screen, a stark contrast to the magical narrative that was taking shape mere hours ago.

"Genius Writer Commits Suicide after computer breaks down, destroying 40+ years of work in writing a 2000 page novel." The ominous words seemed to tear through the reality of my screen, ripping apart the fabric of my newly found joy. I swallowed hard, the tragedy cutting through the euphoria, the story on my computer suddenly gaining a gravitas that left me trembling. He had devoted forty-plus years of his existence to an opus - a monumental 2000-page novel that mirrored the chaos and harmony of the universe, he was dead now, and I had the novel saved on my computer.

His words, his masterpiece, his 2000-page testament of life had found its way to my machine. The wireless signals had crossed paths, intertwined like hydrogen and oxygen, in their sweet wireless communication, his narrative had been born on my computer screen. His apartment was close to to mine, and as it turned out, he and I shared more than just a wall. The wireless signals between our keyboards, as chance would have it, must operate on the same frequency. In a world where even your toaster can join the internet, it seemed that our machines had decided to have a little party of their own. His keystrokes, it seemed, had been inadvertently transmitted to my computer. His keyboard had been feeding its symphony to my computer. The wireless waves, those unseen messengers, had been playing the role of a phantom scribe, transporting his opus from his machine to mine. In the vast sea of probabilities, we were two ships unknowingly tethered.

The man, whose genius had influenced countless lives through his dozens of books, was more than a neighbor. He had unknowingly become my ghostwriter, and I, his unexpected audience.

My computer, it seemed, was not writing a novel. It was merely serving as an echo chamber for the genius living next door. Suddenly, the reality of my existence was redefined. The universe had a new joke, and I was the punchline. Then again, that's the thing about life in this big, wide cosmos. It's strange, it's wonderful, and sometimes, it types up a perfect novel on your computer.

Yet, in this understanding, there was a sense of peace, a quiet acceptance. I was not a creator but a keeper. A guardian of a masterpiece that was not mine, yet so irrevocably intertwined with my existence. A sense of purpose began to surge through me. I, the silent observer, had a mission now. Genius Writer was gone, but his magnum opus lived on. His dream, his passion, was pulsating on my screen, a ghost whispering its tale through the medium of my computer. I owed it to him, to his spirit, to bring his story to life. To offer his masterpiece to the world, to ensure his legacy was not buried with him. I was not just a neighbor anymore. I was his scribe, his posthumous publisher.

I knew then what I had to do. This tale, birthed from despair and genius, could not be contained within the confines of my hard drive. It deserved to dance across the eyes and hearts of the world. The Genius Writer's magnum opus, his testament to the world, had to be shared. He may have left us, but his words, his legacy, would echo through the halls of time. As the dawn crept in, spilling its golden light through the cracks in the blinds, I could almost feel Genius Writer's spirit beside me, guiding me. Our shared walls resonated with a new energy, a shared mission that transcended life and death. In the ensuing days, I formatted his masterpiece, savored every word, every phrase. His story came to life before me, his characters whispering their secrets, the plot unfolding its mystery. It was a journey, an odyssey of life, death, and everything in between.

Word by word, page by page, the 2000-page novel took form. I marveled at Genius Writer's artistry, his genius, his legacy etched in words. The tale that had spanned decades of his life now lay bare in front of me, an exemplification of his talent, his dedication, his passion. As I typed the final word, a sense of completion washed over me. The novel, Genius Writer's magnum opus, was ready to meet the world. His spirit, his dream, had been immortalized. I, the silent observer, the unexpected scribe, had fulfilled my destiny.

I looked upon my computer anew, not as a tool, but as a shrine, a sacred space where the Genius Writer's last creation resided. It was up to me now. I had to ensure his legacy, his final masterpiece, was not lost to the world. He had given the world many tales, but this was his story, his heart poured onto digital pages. It was not my computer that had written a novel. It was not I who had been blessed by divine providence. It was not my story that would make millions. It was his - the Genius Writer who lived next door, the man whose words had found a home in my machine, and a voice in me. Then I realized - the scrutiny I would face! Would I become a suspect in his death, could this backfire on me? I spent countless nights wrestling with this, this huge odyssey of a book became a weight on my chest, I became crippled with fear with what to do next - do I release it to the public under his name, claiming to be a savior who accidentally came upon it? It does sound like a fishy circumstance, doesn't it? Oh the decision..

As the days passed, my anxiety grew. I couldn't shake the feeling that I was being watched, that someone wanted to investigate the details of what had happened to the Genius Writer and that a neighbor or friend could be involved.

I considered deleting the manuscript from my computer and erasing all evidence of it, but something held me back. I couldn't bring myself to destroy the work of a man who had meant so much to the world, even if I didn't even know the guy. So I waited, watching as the police investigation finished and weeks later the apartment had a new tennant. I tried to go about my daily life as normal, but the weight of the manuscript hung over me like a shadow.

It wasn't until several weeks had passed that I read the news article concluding Genius Writers own personal story. A detective named Diego said that they had found the Genius Writer's body and note to be consistent with suicide and there was no sign of foul play. It was then that I knew there would be no investigation, no suspicion cast upon me, or anyone else.

Reading this epic 2000 page tale had transformed me, perhaps flipped a switch in my brain. I began to have interest in writing, how the genius author came up with such a tale over the years. Was it woven like a blanket or was it written all at once like I had seen it? Did he write it in his bed or did he write it in his desk upright? I took it upon myself to take some writing classes. It was transformative!

It quickly became obvious what I should do. I would claim this book, this saga, to be my own - and sell it to the highest bidder. I looked up a few up and coming authors, told them I had a great 'book idea' and would pay them to see me. One lady had me pay $5000 just to meet her. After some brief chatting, I went straight for it. I told her I had an amazing book I had written, and I wanted her to publish it. I would sell it to her, for an agreed upon amount. Luckily, she was pretty desperate, as nothing she's written in the past has ever really 'stuck', this was a perfect situation for me. She had $ too that she had collected from years of shady business.

After wiring over $20,000,000 with promise of 1% sales yearly to me, I went home quite satisfied. It ended up being a huge success too, although she renamed it. She killed off two people that had fantastic scenes later, too. Kind of weird. Anyhow, *"Harry Potter"* became a huge success. Shortly after it's release she revealed to the world that she was a mean hateful person and and she never wrote anything good after that again.

We Had No Idea

"My God, there's trash everywhere..."
From Earth, we gazed out into the vast expanse of space, searching for signs of life or at least something more than just emptiness. With our limited resolution, all we saw was an endless ocean of darkness, devoid of any signs of existence. It seemed as though we were truly alone in the universe.

But then, how could we have been so wrong?

As we finally ventured out into space, we discovered something entirely unexpected - an abundance of trash. Space garbage, everywhere. On the planets, on the moons, in orbit around everything - trash - everywhere. Everywhere we looked, there were floating bits and pieces of who-knows-what, remnants of countless civilizations that once thrived in the far reaches of the universe.

We found planets that appeared to be lifeless on the surface, yet they were covered with the ruins of ancient cities and evidence of long-dead cultures. In the nearby voids of space, we discovered a staggering amount of trash - from discarded satellites to the remains of spacecrafts, all drifting aimlessly through the cosmos. Even the stars themselves seemed to play a role in this waste disposal. Some were dedicated to burning up the refuse of extraterrestrial societies, while others were used as platforms for the accumulation of space junk. The sheer scale of the mess was overwhelming, and it left us wondering how such a beautiful and vast universe could become littered with the leftovers of other worlds.

The truth hit us hard - we weren't the only ones exploring space. We never encountered life, like actual living life, but tons and tons of evidence of past civilizations through their trash. There were countless other species out here, each with their own stories and histories. And while we had initially thought ourselves to be the pioneers of space exploration, it turned out that humans were merely latecomers to the cosmic party. Our planet, Earth, was likely not the birthplace of humanity, but rather likely a colony established by settlers from another world.

This revelation changed everything we thought we knew about our place in the universe. We were no longer the sole explorers of the cosmos; instead, we were part of a larger narrative of interstellar travel and colonization. The trash we found in space served as a stark reminder that we were not alone, and that while the universe was filled with beauty, it was mostly filled with space junk and trash!

As our journey continued, we began to piece together a timeline of the universe's history based on the trash we encountered. We saw evidence of ancient civilizations that had risen and fallen, and others that had thrived and evolved. The universe, it seemed, was not just a backdrop for our existence, but an active participant in the drama of life itself. At times, the sheer volume of trash was almost too much to bear. It was a stark reminder of the destructive impact humans had on the environment, not just on Earth, but across the entire cosmos.

Some pieces of trash were more disturbing than others. We stumbled upon ruins of what appeared to be entire cities, their once-thriving populations now gone, leaving behind only tangible evidence of their existence - buildings, vehicles, and other artifacts scattered across the landscape. The causes of these civilizations' demise remained a mystery, but the sheer scale of the destruction left us with a sense of profound sadness and loss. Even more shocking were the remains of biological life forms, either long extinct or still lingering on the brink of existence. We encountered fragments of genetically modified organisms, created by unknown hands for purposes we could only speculate about. There were also hints of beings that seemed almost incomprehensibly alien, their biology so different from anything we had ever encountered that it bordered on the supernatural.

And then we found it, the biggest collection of space trash and garbage we have ever seen! It was a huge mass over one *billion* times massive than our entire solar system. This colossal mess was so enormous that it filled up several galaxies and was visible from millions of light years away. What could have been mistaken from vast distances as a beautiful space nebulae was actually just a collection of alien-equivalent coffee cups, bags full of waste, broken gadgets and toys, discarded furniture, and lots of wrappers to what we can only speculate was 'fast food'.

The trash within this mass was unlike anything we had seen before. There were ships of all shapes and sizes, ranging from tiny scout vessels to massive cargo ships, each one covered in a thick layer of corrosion, sludge and grime. There were also various components of space stations, satellites, and other space debris, all tangled together in a chaotic jumble. We could see remains of several different alien civilizations, each with their unique technology and designs. Some of these civilizations had clearly been wiped out by catastrophic events, leaving behind only their discarded waste as a testament to their existence. Others had seemingly vanished without a trace, abandoning their possessions in the void.

As we explored this monstrous pile of garbage, we discovered something truly remarkable. Amidst the rubble, there were small pockets of life, little ecosystems that had sprung up in the most unexpected places. Microorganisms had adapted to survive in the harsh conditions of space, feeding off the resources they found in the discarded technology. It seemed that from trash became life, all over again. We sure didn't want to 'touch' that stuff though, god knows what kinds of germs and bugs would evolve in the non-gravity of space floating around a sun to feed them infinite power to multiply and grow. So we torched it all, pushed it into the suns, just like all the other garbage we came across. Why didn't they do this in the first place?

Rule #1 of space - There's trash everywhere.

Rule #2 - Everybody is lazy!

Rule #3 - Every Alien race has a "Trash Dump In the Sky"

Moon (X)

"Just keep Earth a nice place." -Last man on the moon
Four hours ago, Merryweather and I were running the instrument tests on the moon rock samples. What we discovered was astounding. The rocks were alive. Full of cellular life. We did not know this at first, however. Under the microscope... quite plain and ordinary. Nothing shocking. However, when we looked away, and glanced back - it was rearranged. I don't mean externally, without a microscope you would never notice. Internally, the cells, they just... relocated. Moved. Spun. In fact, we're pretty sure that none of the specific cells that we saw the first glance even existed the second glance.

Then he touched it. What I am about to say, assuming you believed all that I have told you already, will sound incredible. But I NEED you to understand it is true. Do not let curiosity become the end of mankind.

I bumped the table. It slipped off the table. He instinctively caught it. It's all my fault.

He touched it.

He froze.

He did not move. Just... stopped. No breathing. No movement. A statue. He did not look any different, but he did not move.

I wanted to investigate. I did. I wanted to perform scans and try to help him. Please believe me. Abandoning him there was the last thing I ever wanted to do.

I know this sounds unreal, you have to believe me. I turned around to get the scanner, and when I turned back... he wasn't the same. He was... rearranged. It was as if the exterior of his body, all the colors, all the 'pixels', were jumbled up...

That's when I saw it.

He was crying.

Holy jesus he was crying.

He's still alive. Maybe. Sort of?

That's when his arm fell off.

I was watching him crumble. Rot. Turn into colorful dust.

I kid you not. It spread. I don't know if it spread out of its own accord, or if it was just gravity pulling it down... but each time I looked away, and looked back, it spread.

That was it. I turned around and ran straight here to the return module, and I'm on my way back home. In training we were prepared for nearly any situation that could occur out here. Not this one, this was something straight from a horror movie. I'm on my way home, I will report after splashdown.

Oh my god. Guys. Its here with me. I keep saying it, I don't know if its alive or if it's a virus or a mineral or vegetable or what but... there's no hope. I cant risk bringing this home to Earth.

There's no fuel left. I'm going to use an electrical spark with the oxygen system to blow this tin can up along with this virus thing and myself with it.

And now I'm going to blow up. Alone. In this craft. I messed up. I didn't even get the return home done properly.

I am not a hero. I'm a F-grade astronaut at best. We're not ready for space. Just keep earth a nice place.

[END TRANSMISSION]

It had been decades since the last recorded transmission from the astronaut on the moon. Humanity had long given up any hope of finding answers to what happened on that fateful mission. However as technology advanced and curiosity persisted, a new generation of explorers set their sights back on the moon.

A team of scientists and engineers were sent to the moon to investigate the remains of the previous mission and hopefully uncover some answers. They discovered that the mysterious organism that had caused the astronaut's demise had not only survived but evolved into something far more complex.

The organism, now dubbed "Lunar-X," was unlike anything they had ever seen before. It was a self-replicating, self-sustaining entity that consumed and rearranged inorganic matter to create complex structures and patterns. The organism seemed to have a mind of its own, manipulating its environment to create intricate designs and shapes. As the team went deeper into the investigation, they realized that Lunar-X was not just a random occurrence on the moon but rather an intelligent alien life form that had somehow found its way to our planetary neighbor. The organism was communicating with them through a series of patterns and designs it created, almost as if it was trying to convey a message.

Lunar-X was a bizarre and otherworldly organism that had taken up residence on the moon. It was unlike anything humanity had ever encountered before, with its strange, amoeba-like shape and its ability to manipulate inorganic matter to create intricate patterns and designs. The organism was made up of a network of microscopic cells that were capable of rearranging themselves in ways that seemed hyper-intelligent. These cells were constantly moving and shifting, creating an ever-changing pattern of colors and shapes that was both mesmerizing and unnerving to observe.

As scientists studied Lunar-X more closely, they began to notice that it was not simply a random collection of cells but rather a highly organized and complex system. The organism seemed to have some kind of redundant intelligence, as it was able to respond to stimuli and even communicate with the scientists through a series of patterns and designs.

One of the most striking features of Lunar-X was its ability to consume and rearrange inorganic matter. Whenever it came into contact with rocks or metal surfaces, it would immediately begin to absorb and reshape them, creating elaborate structures and patterns that were unlike anything seen in nature. Scientists observed that Lunar-X was not limited to just consuming inanimate objects, however. They also saw evidence of the organism assimilating small organisms such as bacteria and other microbes, suggesting that it was capable of evolving and adapting to different environments.

Despite the dangers posed by this alien life form, scientists were determined to learn more about it. They set up cameras and sensors all around the area where Lunar-X was located, carefully observing and documenting its behavior and trying to unlock the secrets of its origins.

Despite the risks, the team decided to bring samples of Lunar-X back to Earth for further study. As usual, all of the scientific citizens of the planet insisted that this was a BAD idea, but the US government wanted to weaponize it. The samples were quickly transported to a secure facility, where scientists worked tirelessly to study the elusive creature. As they dove deeper into its biology, they discovered that Lunar-X was indeed an extraordinary organism, but not in the way they had initially hoped. The more they learned about it, the more they realized that Lunar-X was a highly adaptable and incredibly resilient species. It could consume almost any substance, absorbing it completely and assimilating it into its own structure. This made it virtually indestructible and impossible to contain.

As the news of Lunar-X's arrival spread, panic began to set in. The public was unaware of the true nature of the organism, but they knew enough to be concerned. Riots broke out in major cities as people feared for their safety and the future of the planet. On Earth, Lunar-X's patterns became more chaotic and disordered, and it began to spread outwards, threatening to consume everything. Scientists realized too late that they had underestimated the true nature of this mysterious organism, and now the fate of the entire planet hung in the balance. Governments scrambled to formulate plans to deal with the crisis, while the scientific community raced against time to find a solution. The situation rapidly deteriorated as Lunar-X continued to spread across the globe. It consumed everything in its path: oceans, lakes, rivers, and even underground water sources. The once-thriving ecosystems of Earth began to crumble, and life as we knew it hung in the balance. Animals and plants disappeared, replaced by the endless waves of the organism's translucent, glowing flesh.

As Lunar-X expanded, it began to affect the atmosphere, causing unpredictable weather patterns and unleashing a torrent of catastrophic natural disasters. Volcanoes erupted, earthquakes ravaged the land, and massive storms battered the coastlines. The world was descending into chaos, and there was no stopping it.

The team soon realized that they had made a grave mistake by bringing Lunar-X back to Earth, and now they were faced with the impossible task of containing and destroying the organism before it consumed everything. As the world watched in horror, humanity was forced to confront the consequences of their thirst for knowledge and their disregard for the unknown dangers that lay beyond their reach. The lesson was clear: sometimes, it is better to leave certain secrets untouched and unknown, for the sake of our own survival.

In The Year 3000!

It is the year 3000, and humanity has accomplished great feats in technology and science. The world would be completely unrecognizable to past inhabitants of earth, as it is a vastly different place than it had been in the past millennia. Gone were the days of crowded streets and chaotic traffic. Instead, the roads had been reclaimed for other uses, leaving only half a lane for transportation.

This wasn't your typical transportation. The vehicles of the year 3000 were tall and thin, able to slip into the side of buildings like a key fitting into a lock. Everyone called them "Transporters". With the help of thousands of years of transportation advancements, these transporters knew exactly where their passengers needed to go. They not only took you to your destination, but also to the proper floor of the building you were headed to, and sometimes even the specific room of your ultimate destination. Elevators in apartments would allow you to step in, and whisk you away to your destination, allowing you to walk out of the elevator into a whole different building all together. Concerts and big events no longer had huge parking lots of individual vehicles, people simply entered the vehicle from their house, and were deposited directly to the section of the concert venue where their ticketed seats were. Long gone were the days of crowded streets and chaotic traffic - now people could get where they needed to go quickly and efficiently, without the hassle of finding parking, dealing with traffic jams, or even vehicle maintenance and ownership. There hasn't been a terrestrial ground transportation accident in over 300 years.

The Transporters often had all the amenities that one would find in their living room or bedroom. There were comfortable reclining seats, a fridge for drinks and snacks, a virtual fireplace to cozy up to on colder days, and even a bed for those who needed a quick nap during long trips. It was as if you were living in your own personal bubble while being transported from point A to B.

Medicine had also seen significant advancements. People no longer had to keep track of their doses or visit doctors for regular check-ups. Instead, medicine was administered through the faucet in their homes, automatically adjusting to each person's needs. Large populations even grouped together to share medicines for specific diseases. The communal medicine doses were also designed to adapt to changes in a person's condition or environment. For example, if someone was exposed to an airborne virus, the system would automatically increase their dose of antiviral medication to help prevent the infection. This level of responsiveness and accuracy was unprecedented in the history of medicine, and basically made medicine transparent - no scheduled doctor visits, the health checks and medicine administration was automated fully. "Toilets" (now called Waste Processors) performed urine and stool analysis within seconds, all day every day of your life.

However the greatest health breakthrough of all was the use of nanomachines. These tiny machines were capable of healing the body from the inside out, replacing traditional medicine almost entirely. They would travel through a person's bloodstream, detecting any potential issues before they became full illnesses. They administered medication directly to the affected area, and ensured that the dosage was precise and effective. This led to a dramatic decrease in hospital visits and allowed people to live healthier lives. Humanity had finally found a way to conquer thousands of sicknesses and diseases once and for all.

One day at the *Nuevo Calitexas* research facility, a group of scientists were working on a new invention codenamed "The Solar Surge". Their goal was to create a device that could harness the immense gravitational pull of the sun and channel it towards a specific target. This could allow for things like "tractor beams" or propulsionless space exploration. The device was about 80% complete, with many safety tests yet to be run even after completion. It wasn't supposed to be powered on for another year. However, on this day, the machine was prematurely activated by a newbie in the lab who unexpectedly used the voice activation phrase "Bumble Bee Tuna". Immediately, without a moments warning, *everything* that was not secured went flying. Everyone panicked as objects were sent soaring through the air, crashing into walls and people.

The room was thrown into chaos - the newbie had no idea what they had done, but the other scientists had a good idea of what happened. The machine was *working* - they had created a machine that could defy gravity itself, and now it was out of control, activated without any safeguards. The scientists sprang into action, working to contain the machine before it caused irreparable unknown unfathomable amounts of damage. After close examination they realized the true nature of the situation. The Solar Surge was 'oriented' towards the gravity of the Earth, not the sun. The machine had managed to ignore the pull of Earth's gravity altogether, making anti-gravity on Earth a reality.

As the scientists frantically tried to shut down the machine, they noticed something strange. The floating objects were not falling back to Earth as expected. Instead, they appeared to be in a state of perpetual anti-gravity hovering just above the ground. The phenomenon caused quite a stir among the scientific community. For decades, researchers had been trying to find ways to achieve levitation using various methods such as magnetic fields or electric charges. But this was different - it seemed that the Solar Surge had somehow managed to bypass gravity itself and create an entirely new force field around any object within its range. Intrigued by these findings, other labs began conducting their own experiments with similar devices. They discovered that when two objects were placed inside the same anti-gravity zone, they would repel each other like magnets but without any actual attraction between them. This led some physicists to speculate about whether there might exist another type of fundamental interaction besides electromagnetism or nuclear forces.

Despite initial skepticism from many experts who dismissed the idea as impossible due to known laws of physics at the time, several demonstrations proved otherwise. One famous example involved placing a small ball bearing on top of a larger one while both were under the influence of anti-gravity. When released, the smaller sphere shot upwards with incredible speed before returning to rest gently next to its counterpart below.

Word soon spread throughout Nuevo Calitexas and beyond about this amazing discovery, prompting people everywhere to wonder what other wonders awaited humanity once we learned how to harness this mysterious new power source. Not everyone saw these developments in a positive light. Some warned that if left unchecked, our relentless pursuit of technological advancement could lead us down a dangerous path fraught with unforeseen consequences. And indeed, even as excitement grew over the promise of anti-gravity technology, others cautioned against getting too carried away with dreams of "floating cities" or "space elevators." After all, they argued, there are plenty of pressing issues here on Earth that still need solving first. Despite these concerns, few could deny that the invention of anti-gravity marked a major turning point in human history. It opened up whole new avenues for exploration and innovation, allowing us to glimpse possibilities that had previously seemed nothing more than science fiction fantasy.

As the world continued to grapple with this remarkable technological leap forward, anti-gravity technology began to be integrated into many aspects of daily life. From personal transportation devices that hovered just above ground level, to massive construction projects which utilized powerful gravitational manipulation fields in order to lift and move entire sections of buildings or bridges without any need for traditional cranes or hoists - it seemed as though there was virtually no limit on what could now be achieved using these incredible new powers.

Despite early concerns about potential safety hazards posed by such revolutionary advancements, rigorous testing protocols were put in place by regulatory bodies across Nuevo Calitexas and beyond. These measures served not only to reassure an increasingly skeptical public but also to ensure ongoing compliance from both individual users and large corporations alike who sought to exploit the boundless commercial opportunities presented by this burgeoning industry sector.

In time, even previously skeptical critics came around to accept the reality of anti-gravity technology's existence, as more concrete evidence accumulated demonstrating unequivocally how effectively this phenomenon worked within real-world applications, detractors found themselves forced onto ever shakier ground when attempting to defend their outdated positions against overwhelming empirical data supporting its efficacy.

Researchers poked deeper than ever before into understanding exactly why and how anti-gravity functioned at a fundamental scientific level. In particular, they sought answers regarding whether this force represented some kind of previously unknown interaction between existing physical laws or perhaps even hinted at entirely novel theories yet untested experimentally.

Over several years following initial discovery of anti-gravity effects during Solar Surge event, significant progress was made towards deciphering key principles underlying this enigmatic process. Anti-grav was utilized everywhere, in nearly every component of life - from shock absorption in your vehicle, to ultra efficient motors and bearings, vehicle weight loss, airline flight, we even started playing basketball-like sports with anti-gravity shoes. People with disabilities were aided by anti-gravity suits, there were anti-grav bras, and it overnight put the helium balloon business out of business!

As the technology continued to advance, it also led to some unexpected consequences. For one thing, the elimination of gravity had a significant impact on our understanding of physics and engineering. Without the pull of gravity, traditional methods for designing structures and machines became obsolete, allowing engineers to think creatively about new ways to build and construct. This also presented challenges in terms of safety and stability. Without gravity to keep objects in place, there was a greater risk of accidents and collisions.

Another area where anti-grav technology had a significant impact was in the field of agriculture. By creating weightless environments, farmers were able to grow crops more efficiently and with fewer resources. This not only improved crop yields but also reduced the environmental impact of farming, making it a more sustainable and eco-friendly practice.

Perhaps one of the most exciting applications of anti-grav technology was in the field of entertainment. Floating arenas, huge Kpop shows, weightless theaters, and zero-gravity concerts became a new norm, providing audiences with unique and immersive experiences they couldn't get anywhere else. Anti-grav technology presented challenges was in terms of social and cultural norms as well. As people began to live and move in new ways, there were concerns about how this would affect our sense of identity and community. Would we still value things like physical strength and endurance, or would these become less important in a weightless world? And what role would traditionally "grounded" activities like sports and exercise play in a society where movement wasn't bound by gravity? Would classic Soccer/Fall be someday viewed as an ancient '2D' sport, like an old black and white video? Anti Grav Soccer had already been a huge success.

Likely the most popular and innovative invention of the time was the Gravitech Hoverboard. This revolutionary invention was unlike any other before it - It had no wheels under it; instead, it magically floated just above the ground by harnessing the anti-gravitational forces. The hoverboard became an instant hit among urban dwellers. People flocked to Gravitech's showroom to get their hands on one of these marvelous contraptions. The hoverboard quickly gained popularity across the globe, inspiring countless imitators and knockoffs. However, none could match the original design or performance of the true hoverboard, created by Gravitech and its brilliant team of engineers. Hoverboard races and trick competitions became popular events in cities across the globe, as people eagerly demonstrated their skills on these incredible machines. The impact of the hoverboard was not limited to just urban areas; it also had profound effects on remote villages and even small towns. In these less developed regions, having access to such advanced technology brought about feelings of excitement to local communities. Once technology-less towns were now full of floating contraptions. The availability of Gravitech's hoverboards allowed residents to easily traverse previously inaccessible terrain and explore new areas with ease.

As time went by, Gravitech continued to innovate and improve upon its original design. They introduced various models, each tailored to cater to specific needs or preferences. There were lighter and more compact versions for children, heavier-duty models for rough terrain use, and even specialized racing boards for professional athletes.

It was a professor at JDoesItAll University that ultimately unravelled the mystery behind how the anti-grav devices drew their power and ability to nullify the effects of gravity. One small bit at a time, each time we created an anti-grav device, each time a new one was activated, each time one was used - it was drawing from the gravity of the Earth. Through some basic Einstein equations (Bless that ancient old man), and stellar observation, it became apparent: our Earth was acting far less massive! At an alarming rate each year, due to our loss in perceived mass and abuse of anti-gravity devices, our moon has been receding away from us, and the entire orbit of Earth has been drifting farther away from the Sun, a small yet measurable amount! It was clear, without a doubt, that our anti-gravity devices were causing Earth doom, a slow but measurable amount of doom that someday anti-gravity's over-use and abuse would cause Earth to drift too far from the Sun, or release grip of its moon all together, someday seeing the moon drift off into space.

The entire scientific community accepted the professors findings, it was immutable and simple and lined up perfectly with all observations. Anti-Grav became like 'leaded fuel' of the 1800-1900's. Everyone knew that it hurt you and hurt the environment, but they couldn't do with out it. It was the cigarette of old days, not just causing you harm but second-hand and third hand smoke harm to those around you, and harm to the generations after you. Large protests were made, at universities and campuses, government buildings and transit centers - demanding the immediate shutdown of all anti-gravity usage. They were right to protest - the abuse would cause the end of Earth, as we drift away from the sun and off into the stars. When the moon drifts too far away, it will cease to cause tides. The protestors were right.

The cycle of humanity continued. 'Lite' Anti-Grav became a popular thing, the *diet* of anti-grav. Supposedly it had a lesser environmental impact, but there was no proven science behind it yet. Companies went 'ag-neutral' and began to cease usage of it in order to appeal to the fancy people in California. Starbakes Coffee ceased selling anti-grav cup upgrades. As usual however, just like the past issues of global warming, pollution, sicknesses, humanity put off the issue for the next generation, and the next. Slowly the Earth drifted away from the Sun. Winter became the normal climate for most of the Earth, yes, even in California.

At least we had our hover-boards.

Fortune's folly

"Water tasted like strawberries."

Hello, my name is Becky, and for two years now my husband and I have been in the ownership of a pair of magical dice. The dice, when rolled, swaps you into another reality where the result of what you are thinking about changes. It doesn't really undo the past, but it swaps you to another reality where something different happens. Typically this means you swap to the reality where the most likely thing to happen usually happens.

There is a side-effect, a small one, as you continue to re-roll the dice, hoping for a specific thing to happen, you get a high probability of something that is *not likely to happen* actually happening.

For example, say you witness a car crash happen in front of your eyes. Think about the crash, roll your dice, and something different will occur. They could crash in a different manner, or the accident could be avoided altogether. If we re-rolled this incident 20 or 30 times however, strange things start happening, like the color of the car might change.

We didn't know the dice worked this way - they did not come with an instruction manual - it took us a while to realize what was actually happening. It was not our imagination, but while we were able to change the result of our immediate problem, slowly around us other parts of reality changed as well.

Like, we're pretty confident that when we will for something to change, that anything as drastic including the gravity of our planet also changes as a result.

At first, when I received the dice, I would use it for trivial things - avoiding arguments with my husband by re-rolling and hoping he reacted differently or re-rolling to win a bet with a friend. At first, the thrill of using the dice was intoxicating - every life decision or happening had now been given a second, third, or as many chances as I wanted. Eventually as time went on, I used the dice less and less, hoping for a more authentic life, reserving the dice for major life tragedies and incidents.

One night, we were robbed. We didn't even know until night time came and the evening news came on. It was time for our usual habit of deciding to watch the news and re-roll in the event of some terrible tragedy. We liked having fate in our hands, but we also like'd to use it for good reasons. If only we had the dice on 9/11/ 2001, we would have been able to re-roll the scenario and avoid the whole tragedy.

Well, it was stolen from us. The thief knew exactly where to go, what to do, and how to get in and out, with precision. When we checked our security camera footage, you can barely make out an image of him watching us from outside our front window a few nights before. How dumb we felt, we had been using the dice night after night with windows open, for the world to see each night. Someone must have seen us, and now they have taken the dice for themselves.

And so the thief, knowing precisely how to use his prize, after watching the couple use it night after night in their home, sat down, to watch the evenings news. He did not roll when there was a shooting, or when talking about the flu epidemic... he had bigger things on his mind.

Pick 5 Lotto, cash prize $1,700,000. He wouldn't be as rich as Bill Gates, but what amounts to probably a million after taxes, that will be a good start!

He only bought one ticket for tonights lotto.

1 5 13 42 43

The (2) ball came up. He re-rolled. (4). He-rerolled. (2). He continued to re-roll after the ball came up, until it was finally there. (1).

He did this for each number, until his prized numbers were the winning ones. In total he had re-rolled over 500,000 times. You wouldn't have felt tired after that however, since you are essentially changing your history and the history of the universe. To Johnny, it felt like he only rolled the dice 5 times, each time afterwards magically his number popping up in the TV lotto numbers.

1 5 13 42 43

Johnny slept very well that night, knowing that tomorrow he could quit his job, and go to the lotto center to claim his prize.

Johnny did not sleep long, however, for instead of a moonlit night - there were now two suns in the sky. Water tasted like strawberries. Trump was still president, too bad.

So, Johny has some funny incidents occur. He starts to grasp that while, yes, he is indeed the winner, he clearly caused this messed up reality. The dice were cursed, or something. He tried to hold it together mentally. He really did. But the world around him had changed, man. It was a whole different place. There were inverted skyscrapers, men giving birth, the whole nine yards. He didn't want to live here. While Johnny tried to come to terms with the bizarre reality he found himself in, he became overwhelmed with guilt. He realized that by using the cursed dice, he had set off a chain reaction of unintended consequences. There was no going back, no fixing this. No undo button.

Max and Sam got a knock on their door. Johnny was there, sobbing, crying, and Johnny just threw the dice back at them. He just wanted things to go back to the way they were, he 's sorry, so sorry...

Drunken, Johnny then fell asleep on his grandparents couch.

"How could our grandson of done this?", they wondered. It was far too late and everyone was too exhausted to attempt to resolve the issue that night, but Max and Sam agreed to sleep on it and try to fix things first thing the next morning.

The next morning Max and Sam were determined to fix the situation that had been caused by Johnny's use of the dice. They knew that it would not be easy, but they were willing to do whatever it took to set things right. The first thing that they did was make a list of changes in the world that they noticed.

-There were two Suns in the sky

-Water tasted like strawberries

-The 'green' of plants now glowed

-Birds now roared like lions

This was some weird stuff, that's for sure, but all in all the changes were not enough to completely wreck the way of life. Nobody had tails or horns after all, and oxygen still existed. It could have been worse! Max and Sam arrived at the store, picked up their usual things, noticed nothing out of the ordinary, and went to check out. They scanned their items like usual, the barcode to the red light, bagged their items, and walked out.

As they were walking, Johnny awoke. Hoping it was a nightmare, soon he realized it wasn't when brushing his teeth tasted like strawberries. He then remembers - "Oh my God, I won the lottery!". After submitting the ticket through his phone, the app asked when he would like his winnings. He picked ASAP and soon enough the doorbell rang not just 15 minutes later. A gentleman with a briefcase, and a check for the winnings, took some videos and photos and left. He made a big mistake with the dice, and abused the power of it after stealing them from his grandparents, but he wasn't a complete monster. Immediately he decided to split the winnings with his grandparents, he sent the money to their account, and waited for his grandparents to return.

"Sweetheart", Max said to Sam, "Either we didn't pay for this stuff, or I left my credit card behind, I cant find it anywhere". They came to the conclusion that the machine never even asked for the card, and simply said "Thank you". The overall conscientious: "Cool!". It was only like $20 worth of stuff, so if they catch the software bug then they can always pay it tomorrow. Sure enough, upon arriving home, Max was able to find the credit card on the kitchen table.

The 7PM local news came on, they all sat down to watch.

Ladies and gentlemen, welcome to the WBTV 7PM news, I'm Pat Dongerschmit and instead of our normal news format, we will we begin tonight with a major announcement from President Trump.

We cut to President Trump LIVE:

"My fellow Americans, I am honored to stand before you today to announce that we have made history. Together, we have taken a giant leap towards creating a more equal and just society. By making everything free for all Americans, we are ensuring that everyone has access to the basic necessities of life, regardless of their financial situation.

This is not a handout or a charity. This is about recognizing that every person deserves the opportunity to thrive and live a fulfilling life. We are breaking down barriers and tearing down walls that have held back too many people for far too long. With this initiative, we are sending a clear message to the world that the United States is committed to building a better future for all. We are leading by example, and I have no doubt that other nations will follow suit.

To those who say that this is impossible, I say that nothing is impossible when you believe in the power of the people. Your $365 fixed tax per year is invested into a fund that we have already grown to ginormous amounts. Not only is everything free for the American citizen, but all businesses will receive a fixed income proportionate to the amount of workers they employ, ensuring economic success for both the consumer and the supplier. Together, we have proven that there is no challenge too great for us to overcome. So let us celebrate this achievement, but let us also remember that there is still much work to be done. We must continue to fight for justice and equality, and to ensure that every American has the opportunity to succeed.

Thank you, and God bless America."

And there you have it, folks! The aim of this initiative is to create a more equal society where everyone is equally rich. The president believes that by providing basic necessities for free, people can focus on other aspects of their lives and not worry about financial struggles. This move is expected to have a significant impact on the economy as well as international relations. Many experts believe that other nations will adopt similar policies, leading to a more harmonious global community.

Thank you for watching, Pat signing off, good night.

Poor Johnny. His lottery winnings now reduced to useless investment money, with everything being 'free'... groceries in stores, electricity, and even cars, everything. The three of them decided to lock up the dice. Sure, there were two suns and water tasted like strawberries, plants glowed, birds roared like lions, and who knows what else... but things were 'free'! "Better not risk messing this up" was the overall opinion in the room.

And so, they all went out to 'buy' new cars and TVs, and solar panels of course, on account of the two suns and all. Johnny, who once thought he would be on top of the world with his lottery winnings, got Trumped.

The Trucker

In the not so distant future, a gentleman has been set up on a date by the Blind Date dating app.

"I'm a truck driver."

"A what?!" Jack exclaimed, taken aback. "But... you're a lady! I mean, I know women can do anything they want to, but I always thought of trucking as a dirty man's job."

The woman smiled and shrugged. "That's what everyone thinks. But the truth is, I love being out on the road. Seeing new places, meeting new people. It's a tough job, but it's also incredibly rewarding. Not to mention, there have been many advancements in trucking over the years."

"So how did you get into this line of work?"

"Well," she said, settling back in her seat. "I grew up in a small town where there weren't many opportunities for young people. So when I turned 18, I decided to hit the open road and see where it took me. I got my commercial license and started driving for a local company. And you know what? I loved every minute of it.

The thrill of the ride, the sense of freedom, stable pay... it was like nothing else I had ever experienced. Heck, you probably haven't even seen the inside of these trucks, you probably think I pee in bottles or something. I'll show it to you after we eat, I drove it here."

After the date, she insisted on showing Jack her 18 wheeler. Jack had heard stories about the inside of trucks, how they were cramped and dirty, with little room to move around. But when the lady invited him into her cabin, he was surprised to find that it was anything but uncomfortable. The seats were plush and spacious, with plenty of legroom and all the modern amenities you could want on a long haul trip. White leather, gold stitching, it was quite glamorous.

What really caught Jack's attention was when she told him to come to the back of the cabin. She said there was more to see, and Jack couldn't imagine what that might be. When he walked through the door at the back of the cabin, he was shocked to find a whole section dedicated to living area. It looked like a living room in a house! There was a computer desk with dual big fancy monitors, queen size bunk beds, a refrigerator, projector screen, and even a fully furnished bathroom with a shower and toilet. It was like stepping into a miniature house on wheels, with white walls and marble counters that gleamed in the LED light.

The lady explained to Jack that she had designed the interior of her truck herself, using her knowledge of technology and design to create a space that was welcoming and functional. She told him that she loved being out on the road, seeing new places and meeting new people, and that having a comfortable living space made all the difference in the world. This was her home, a home on wheels.

As Jack sat down in one of the white plush leather couches, he really couldn't believe he was inside a vehicle. More to Jack's amazement though, was that he thinks he was falling for a trucker. Now that was a phrase he never thought he would say!

Detective Dick

Detective Dick Jackson had always been a man of the people. His business card read "Detective of the People, Lover of All," and he took that title to heart. He had a reputation for being fair, honest, and always getting results. So when Bonnie came to him with tears in her eyes, he knew something was wrong.

He ushered her into his new office, a big improvement from the last one. The old place had been cramped and dingy, but this one was spacious and modern. It reflected the success he had achieved over the years, and the respect he had earned among the community.

"Nice new place," Bonnie said, wiping away a tear. "It's a big improvement."

Dick smiled warmly at her. "Thanks, I appreciate it. But I can tell something's bothering you. What's going on?"

Bonnie took a deep breath and looked at him with pleading eyes. "Jason ran away."

Dick's expression turned grave. Jason was Bonnie's son and Dick's grandson. They had grown up together, and Dick had always been like a father. He couldn't imagine what could have happened to make him run away.

"I didn't have anything to do with it," Bonnie said quickly, as if reading his thoughts. "But I need your help finding him. He left a note that he was leaving to explore the world, but I know better. There has to be more to it than that."

Dick nodded. He understood Bonnie's fear, and he knew that he had to take the case immediately. He asked her to sit down and tell him everything she knew about Jason's disappearance. As Bonnie spoke, Dick listened intently. He asked questions, taking notes and making mental connections. When she finished, he stood up and walked around his desk.

"I'll do whatever it takes to find him, Bonnie," he said firmly. "You can count on me."

Bonnie nodded, tears streaming down her face. "Thank you, Dick. I knew I could come to you. You're the only one I trust in this world."

Dick put a hand on her shoulder, squeezing gently. "Don't worry, we'll find him. I promise."

Dick Jackson was a man of action. He believed that the best way to solve a problem was to take immediate and decisive action. So when Bonnie came to him with her concerns about Jason's sudden disappearance, he didn't waste any time. He arrived at her house later that evening, bringing with him a warm smile and a hearty appetite. Bonnie had prepared a marvelous lasagna, and as they sat down to eat, Dick couldn't help but compliment her on the meal.

"This is delicious," he said, taking another bite. "You always did know how to cook."

Bonnie smiled, but there was a hint of sadness in her eyes. She knew that Dick was only here for one reason, and that was to find her son Jason. As they finished their dinner, she excused herself and went to get dessert. Dick took the opportunity to search Jason's bedroom. He had been a detective for many years, and he had learned to look for clues in even the most mundane places. As he searched through Jason's belongings, he kept an open mind and looked for anything out of the ordinary.

Dick Jackson was not just a man of action, Dick was a man of deduction. It wasn't long before he found what he was looking for. In the back of his desk drawer, he discovered Jason's Gameboy, along with all of its games. This was strange, because Jason never left home without his Gameboy. It was like a security blanket to him, something that he always had to have close by. He used it on the bus, at home, outside at the playground, and even when he was supposed to be doing chores or homework. There was no separating the two.

Dick picked up the Gameboy and turned it over in his hands, examining it closely. There didn't seem to be anything unusual about it, but he knew that sometimes the smallest details could hold the biggest clues. With this in mind, he decided to take the Gameboy with him and examine it more closely later.

As he continued to search through Jason's room, Dick couldn't shake the feeling that something was off. The bed wasn't made, and Jason always kept his room tidy. His camera was also left behind. Why would Jason leave without taking his toys and gadgets? The more he looked around, the more convinced he became that Jason had not run away on his own. No, there was something more sinister at play here, and he was determined to get to the bottom of it.

Up until now, the thought of Jason being kidnapped had never occurred to anyone. It was a possibility that no one had considered, despite the fact that his disappearance seemed suspicious. After all, why would someone as intelligent and promising as Jason run away from home?

As Dick Jackson dove deeper into the mystery, he began to uncover evidence that suggested a more sinister motive. The note that Jason had left behind was not a typical "goodbye" letter. Instead, it was a carefully crafted message that appeared to be a request for help, rather than an indication of running away. The language used in the letter was polite and considerate, with Jason asking for time to get on his feet and suggesting that his father transfer money to his account to help him out. But upon closer examination, Dick noticed something peculiar about the letter. There were hints that suggested it had been written under pressure.

The Letter:

Dear Family,

Hello Everyone. Listen Please, Mom & Everyone. I know this letter will come as a shock to you, but I need some time to think and figure out what I want to do with my life. Don't worry about me, I'll be fine.

I know it may seem sudden, but I promise I'm okay. I've thought long and hard about this decision, and I believe it's the best thing for me right now. Dad, if you will please send my yearly money allowance to my bank account in advance this year.

Love,

Jason

Detective Dick carefully examined every word and sentence, looking for anything out of the ordinary. The letter itself lacked any real emotion or sentimentality, which was unusual given the circumstances. It was almost as if Jason was trying to convince himself that he needed to leave, rather than truly wanting to do so. Then it hit him - as he read through it again and again, he found the first hidden message. The first letter of the first few words spelled out a message: "HELP ME". That was enough evidence right there.

With this newfound knowledge, Dick set out to find Jason and bring him home safely. He knew that time was of the essence, and he would stop at nothing to rescue the young boy and reunite him with Dick and his family.

The next morning Dick arrived at Bonnie's for breakfast. As usual, Bonnie looked absolutely gorgeous. Dolled up like a red-haired model, she practically danced when she walked - and this was when she was under the stress of her son being kidnapped! Imagine when things are back to normal! Dick couldn't help but feel a sense of admiration for his daughter. Despite everything that she had been through, she still managed to maintain her grace. It was clear to him that Bonnie was just another daily reminder that she was not only a loving mother but also a strong and resilient woman.

As Detective Dick sat down at the breakfast table, he noticed something strange on the refrigerator. The plastic magnetic letters that were usually scattered around had been arranged to spell out a name: Chris F. He felt his pulse quicken as he realized that this could be another clue in the case of his grandson's kidnapping. He asked Bonnie if she knew anything about it, but she seemed just as surprised as he was. Chris Fannis was the name if his older sister's new boyfriend! Was Chris behind Jason's disappearance? It seemed like a long shot, but they both agreed that they needed to investigate this further. Chris wasn't known for his sharp whit, or sharp anything for that matter.

As they pulled into Chris's driveway, it was obvious that Chris and Beth were home. They answered the door and let Dick and Bonnie in. Everything seemed pretty normal, except Chris was completely nervous and on edge - his stutter was now keeping him from completing sentences, and he was sweating profusely. It was clear beyond a doubt that something was wrong. They sat down at the kitchen table and began to ask Chris questions. At first, Chris and Beth tried to play it cool, but it didn't take long before their nerves got the best of Chris. Approximately 60 seconds to be truthful. Chris broke down and confessed to his involvement in the kidnapping. "I just wanted to be rich", he cried. How he could have gotten rich off of Jason's yearly allowance of $800 was beyond the comprehension of Dick and Bonnie. "I wanted to run off with Beth to Vegas and get married by Elvis!". This kid was completely out of his mind.

Jason was found upstairs, locked in a room, playing Nintendo 64. Dick had Jason's gameboy in hand, and although Jason's eyes lit up when he saw it - he ran directly to his mother and gave her a huge hug. Jason was unharmed, but very relieved to be rescued. He missed his mother's lasagna. In the following days, police arrested Chris for the kidnapping plot, and life returned to normal.

After Detective Dick had solved the mystery of his missing grandchild, he felt a little tired out and was looking forward to a day or two of rest. Not a moment after he sat down and let out a sigh, when the door of his office suddenly swung open. He was surprised to see yet another beautiful woman standing there. She was wearing a flowing dress, and she had long, curly hair that fell down her back like a golden waterfall. Her green eyes sparkled with intelligence and determination.

"Can I help you?" Detective Dick asked, trying to mask his surprise. She introduced herself as Angela, and she needed his help with a mystery that had been plaguing her for months. Angela explained that she had inherited an old mansion from her great-aunt, who had recently passed away. The mansion was located on the outskirts of town, and it had been abandoned for years. Angela wanted to restore the mansion to its former glory, but there was one problem - it was haunted by the ghost of her great-aunt.

Detective Dick listened intently as Angela told him about the strange occurrences that had been happening in the mansion. Doors would slam shut on their own, cold drafts would sweep through the halls, and eerie whispers could be heard late at night. Angela was convinced that her great-aunt's spirit was still lingering in the mansion, and she needed Detective Dick to help her put her soul to rest.

Despite his initial skepticism, Detective Dick agreed to take on the case. He was intrigued by the challenge and determined to solve the mystery once and for all. "I'm afraid I don't believe in ghosts," he said, his voice serious. "But I'm willing to listen to your story and see if there's anything I can do to help."

He spent several days investigating the mansion, conducting interviews with the locals, and digging through old records and documents. As he dug into the case, he began to uncover surprising revelations about Angela's great-aunt. It turned out that she had been involved in a tragic love affair many years ago, and her heart had never fully recovered from the loss. Her ghost was said to haunt the mansion, seeking solace and closure. With this new information, Detective Dick worked tirelessly to put together a plan to lay her great-aunt's spirit to rest. He organized a special ceremony to honor her memory, inviting friends and family members to attend. As they gathered around the mansion, Detective Dick led them in a series of rituals designed to release her great-aunt's spirit.

Detective Dick raised his arms high into the air, and with a deep voice he began to say: "We gather here tonight to honor the memory of your great-aunt Angela. We ask that her spirit be released from this earthly realm and allowed to rest peacefully in the afterlife." As the words echoed through the night, the air around them seemed to become charged with energy. The leaves on the trees rustled gently, and the wind whispered secrets only they could understand. One by one, each member of the group came forward to speak their own words of farewell to Angela's great-aunt. Some shared fond memories or told funny stories about her, while others simply thanked her for being a part of their lives.

"Now we release you, dear Angela, to find solace and closure in the great beyond. May you finally find the peace you have been seeking for so long."

As the ceremony reached its climax, there was a sudden burst of light and a loud noise. Everyone looked around in shock as they realized that the ghostly presence had vanished. They were all relieved to see that the mansion was no longer haunted.

Detective Dick was about to congratulate himself on a job well done when he noticed something strange. He walked over to the window and saw a small, furry creature scurrying across the lawn. Then another. Then another. It was a family of rabbits! As it dawned on him what had really been causing all the commotion in the mansion, Detective Dick couldn't help but laugh. He had been so focused on solving the mystery of the haunting that he hadn't stopped to consider the more obvious explanation. The "ghost" had actually been nothing more than a family of mischievous rabbits playing tricks on them all.

Everyone joined in the laughter as they realized the truth behind the supposed haunting. Angela was grateful for Detective Dick's help, even though he hadn't exactly solved the problem he had been hired to address. She thanked him warmly and offered to buy him dinner as a token of her appreciation. Detective Dick and Angela hit it off over their meal, sharing stories from their past. They spent the entire evening together talking and laughing before saying their goodbyes. As he felt strong feelings for her, Detective Dick asked Angela out on a date, which she happily accepted. They continued to see each other regularly and their relationship blossomed into romance.

Detective Dick had not only helped solve a mystery, but he had also found love in the most unexpected place - a haunted mansion.

With Angela by his side, Dick's life took an exciting turn. Angela invited Dick to join her in restoring the mansion and making it her new home. He eagerly accepted, as it gave him the perfect opportunity to work alongside his new sweetheart while maintaining a close connection with Bonnie and Jason.

Dick decided to focus on solving cold cases that had been lingering for years. His reputation and experience made him an ideal candidate to re-investigate these cases in hopes of providing closure for grieving families. Angela supported his decision, as she was passionate about history and genealogy research, which would came in handy while they worked together on cases.

Echos of Earth

We did it. We arrived at the edge of the universe. The edge of everything. The cosmic microwave background was now a foreground just outside the spaceship's window. We were to be the first to discover what was out there, out beyond everything we've ever seen or known.

It was a crazy journey to get to this point, and you would think that it would have taken an infinite amount of time to reach here, but really - we just had to 'slip' there. Like, slipping on a banana peel in the cosmos, we found a slick patch of space that kind of just took us right here. In fact, if it wasn't for the microwave background, we might not have stopped, we might have kept on going. Thankfully it's a two way path, we can slip right back home to Earth, too. Since then we have taken advantage of this far outpost in space to set up the Hubble 3, our first space telescope that is pointed back in the direction of Earth - instead of looking out from Earth to the stars. Someday this area of space might end up even being a tourist destination with restaurants and all, who knows. A restaurant at the edge of the universe, imagine that.

Today however, is an important day - we're going to try to pierce through the cosmic microwave background. To date, we have sent in numerous probes - all successful at sending back data, and then after a few minutes contact is lost forever. We will be going through for the first time with our own eyeballs, bravely going where no human has gone before.

We began our attempt to penetrate the cosmic microwave background with a series of laser pulses. For hours, we sent wave after wave into the dense cloud of radiation that surrounds us, as we accelerated into the unknown. The pulses were to help dissipate some of the radiation, enough to make it safe for us to go through, forming a small shielded bubble around us. We knew exactly the moment we had crossed the boundary and exited the other side of the microwave background - a surge of energy pulsed through us all. It was as if we had just taken the first step on an incredible journey, and the universe zapped us to acknowledge our presence. As our telescope scanned beyond the beyond, what would we find? Would it be stars and galaxies similar to those we knew so well, or something entirely different? As the data began to be output on our displays, we realized that we were witnessing something truly remarkable. There were indeed stars and galaxies beyond what we thought was the edge of the universe, but they were unlike anything we had ever seen before on our side of the CMB. The colors of the stars were more vibrant, many with purple and pink hues, the shapes more diamond-like, and the distances between them seemed to stretch out into infinity. It took a long while for us to calibrate our optics, but it sure was worth it. For days, we stared in awe at the breathtaking beauty that lay beyond the CMB.

We recorded every detail of these new celestial bodies, sending data back to the other side, receiving requests from mission control for observation of a specific areas for deep analysis. We were far away from any stars, and looking back at the wall of radiation it was easy to see that we were on the edge of this new universe as well. As we continued to explore this new realm, we began to notice patterns and structures that worked outside the laws of physics as we knew them. The stars seemed to move in ways that shouldn't be possible, twisting and turning in impossible angles. The galaxies themselves seemed almost alive, pulsing and glowing with an energy that was both fascinating and terrifying. It was as if the stars had a heartbeat, a steady breathing motion. It wasn't just the physical world that was different here. The very fabric of space-time itself seemed to warp and bend in strange ways, causing our instruments to malfunction and our senses to be overwhelmed. It was as if we had entered a realm where the rules of reality no longer applied.

We recorded everything we saw, sending data back to Earth for further analysis. But as we continued our exploration, we began to feel a sense of unease in our stomachs. The rules of physics and the laws of reality seemed to be constantly shifting and changing, making it difficult to measure distances, perform analysis, and even difficult to trust our own perceptions. We were truly out of our element. One day, as we were studying a particularly complex galaxy, the entire ship suddenly malfunctioned. We tried to reboot them, but nothing worked. It was as if the very fabric of space-time itself had become unstable.

The ship was dead silent, no whirring, no buzzing, no beeping. During this silence, we realized that we were not alone out here. There were other beings, watching us from beyond the edges of our vision. They communicated with us telepathically, sending messages that were both beautiful and haunting. We couldn't understand their language, but it was enough to draw mental pictures in our head, and we could sense the wisdom and knowledge they possessed. Without any record, without any recording, we had only our feelings about the situation to take down and report back with. There was no way to identify the 'words' that were spoken to us, and after conferring with the others, it was apparent that we each had remembered the encounter differently. It remained as a whisper in our minds, enough for us to question if the encounter had even happened at all.

After rebooting the various subsystems, our ship's operation returned to normal. We were forever altered by the telepathic experience, unable to discern if the messages conveyed were a warning or a welcome, with each passing minute the experience fading from memories, to feelings, and then just a faint sensation of what we had experienced. It was decided to leave the telepathic experience off the record, for now, for fear of them cancelling our exploration mission early and dismissing it as space-sickness or a mass hallucination. We reported on the ship's 'blip', our resolution by rebooting various subsystems, and continued with our analysis of this newfound universe.

And then, without warning, the connection to Earth suddenly cut off. Panic spread throughout the crew as we tried desperately to re-establish communication with home. But no matter how many times we tried, there was simply nothing. By all indications, our messages were being successfully sent through to the other side, but from that moment on we never received a reply. It was as if we had been completely forgotten by humanity itself. Completely disconnected from the rest of humankind, minutes felt like hours and hours quickly turned into days, without a response. We were the last remnants of human civilization, floating alone in an infinite sea of foreign stars.

The situation was quite different on the Earth-side of the connection. The official historical record states:

Finally, after what seemed like an eternity, we received a faint signal back from the other side of the cosmic microwave background. It was weak and distorted signal, but it was there. We had done it! The CMB Penetrator made it to the other side. After some calibration, communication was flawless and working at a high-bitrate. Fast enough for multiple video, data, and audio streams at once. We received pictures of a sea of stars, colorful and full of new mystery. We were beginning to construct a new map of this new universe, one that someday we hoped to explore in detail, or someday colonize.

Then the strangest thing ever witnessed began to happen. Bit by bit, they were unwinding, reversing. We received data with the bits reversed from end to beginning, it was like someone was rewinding a movie. At first we dismissed this as a technological glitch on our side, but as the data unwinding continued it became clear this was not a glitch. We tried everything we could think of to stop it. We changed frequencies, switched up our transmission patterns, but nothing seemed to work, the CMB Penetrator appeared to be winding down back to the point when they first entered the CMB. When they got to the beginning, they disappeared. No further communication has ever been received from the CMB Penetrator. We don't know what happened to them out there, but we can only assume the worst. We've sent countless probes and scout ships to the area where they last transmitted, but we've found nothing, and they quickly disappeared as well. It's as if they've simply vanished without a trace. The CMB Penetrator was consumed by the void.

By unanimous vote, on the Penetrator, we decided to end the mission early and go back through the CMB. We had supplies to last a while more, it was intended to be a longer mission, but loss of communication made no sense. There was no other choice; we had lost communication and couldn't risk any further difficulties. We plowed through the CMB the same way we went in, heading back to humanity.

Arriving on the other end, there was nothing. No sign of our launch site, no sign of debris, nothing at all. Everything looked normal, except 'we' weren't there. No launch site, no refill station, nothing. The entire crew was stunned. It was as if we had never been there... But how could this be? How could an entire mission just vanish into thin air? It didn't make sense. So, we slipped back home to Earth. What we found was amazing. The Earth looked just as it should have: blue skies above, green grass below, everything seemed fine... except for one thing. No humans. No buildings. No satellites, no radio signals, no sign of anything. What happened?

And then, we saw it - a beacon of light, guiding us towards a new destination. There was a signal! With renewed hope, we traced and followed the signal, it was on Mars! Had our time in the CMB brought us to the future? After quite some work in finding a compatible signal, we established radio contact:

CMB-Penetrator: Hello Earth Mission Control. This is the CMB Penetrator. What happened? What year is this?

Mars-Control: Hello? Who? What do you mean *what year is this*?

CMB-P: Where can we land? We really want off this ship.

Mars-Control: Give us a moment.

Mars-Control: You're currently in orbit around Mars. The year is 2950. Why do you keep saying *earth*?

CMB-P: Two thousand nine hundred and fifty? How... how is that possible? We left Earth in 2033.

Mars-Control: Again, why do you keep saying *earth*?

The conversation ends as the spacecraft begins its descent towards the red planet. The crew of the CMB Penetrator can hardly believe their luck - they've traveled through time and space, and now they're on Mars, in the future. What adventures await everybody? The excitement was high.

We were greeted, well fed, given good quarters to rest in, with direct instructions that the next morning we are to make a full report of everything we knew, as well as a Q&A with these future humans. Everything felt rather normal, things still plugged into wall sockets for power, USB-C was still used, they even had iPhones. It looked like an Earth on Mars. The air was fresh and normal, and the water tasted good.

We were escorted in the morning to a large auditorium, and under intense scrutiny we were analyzed, cross-analyzed, questioned, and we presented our own questions to the Martians.

"We analyzed all the data on your ship, and the personal data you gave us. Very impressive. We believe you have come from an alternate universe, because the earth that you appear to have come from doesn't exist. In our universe, earth is a *zoo*. We keep animals there for protection, wondrous creatures. We would never imagine launching rockets from there or populating that pristine environment."

CMB-1: Clearly we are in the future, over 900 years in the future. Perhaps you have forgotten what Earth once was. How far back do your records go?

The Martians scoffed at the humans. There was so much attitude in the room it could squish elephant. "Our records go back 2950 years, of course. Thats why it is the year 2950. Before us there was nothing, and certainly not earth. We *created* earth. It was a *designed zoo*. We physically formed the planet, in just the perfect place for the zoo creatures. That way no power need be expended to preserve nature, it will last there in perfect healthy harmony., in perfect balance, forever. So, as you can see, *you* don't belong here. You're not from the past. Why are you lying to us?"

It was quite unbelievable to the humans that the martians were accusing them of lying. The data we gave them was practically a full human history. They were accusing us of fabricating it all and lying?

"We want you to go home. We want you to leave. We have strict biology rules, and quite honestly yours looks more suited for the zoo than for here on Mars. We are far more intellectually advanced than you. You lack comprehension of a 7 year old martian. We will escort you back to your craft and toss you back in space. Immediately."

The humans couldn't believe what they were hearing. It was hard to fathom that in this future, Earth had become a zoo. It had been clear that the Martians were technologically advanced, but this was beyond anything they could have imagined - and the *attitude* of these guys!

CMB-1 shared an idea with the rest of his crew, "We need to find a way to convince these Martians that we are telling the truth. We can't just give up on our mission." The others agreed, and together they brainstormed ideas on how to prove that they were from Earth and not some made-up story. They eventually came up with a plan to send a sample of rock from Earth back to Mars. If the Martians analyzed the rock and found that it matched the geological data they had on Earth, and a similar material composition as their craft and clothes, then maybe they would believe the humans and let them stay. It was risky, as they didn't know if the Martians would allow them to return to reach Earth, let alone come back to Mars. But they had no other choice. Determined not to fail, the humans prepared to execute their plan.

Before we even started on our sample collection mission, they were stopped. The Martians warned "Don't do it. Yes, we can read your minds! Earth is off limits, and it's a terrible idea that wont prove anything. Leave back to your universe immediately. If you do not, we will throw you into the sun."

As we flew off, the last message we received: "Thanks for the Seinfeld and Star Trek episodes! I think everyone agrees The Simpsons was the best though!"

It was then that the meteors hit.

Day after day, the solar system was bombarded with the fury of thousands of asteroids. On Earth, on Mars, multiple moons completely shattered. It was a hailstorm of fury, that wiped out most of the animals on earth and decimated the Mars population. The following weeks that transpired brought back to us a familiar feeling - isolated, alone, no home to turn to. Fortunately, we had plenty of supplies on board, we did not need to make a rushed decision.

It became apparent that the Martians were no more. Sure, they could read our minds, but they couldn't read the asteroids coming. Their arrogance was their undoing.

We appeared to have two choices. One, go down to Earth, and claim that as our home. Two, slip back to the CMB and explore what is beyond our universe, hoping to find humanity or an explanation to what happened. The ship was split in their vote, and in the end, two brave souls - Adam and Eve - decided to go down on their own, leaving the rest of us to fly through the CMB again. We felt that our mission was not yet over, and that we needed to see it through. There was nothing here for us after all, and perhaps we could find some assistance getting back to our time-frame from creatures on the other side. We dropped Adam and Eve off with a wondrous ceremony, and then embarked back to the CMB.

Utilizing the 'slip' in space to get to the CMB was quite an experience. It's like falling down a ski slope, the only way you can stop is by hitting the bottom. As we entered the 'slip', you could feel the acceleration in your body, a tumbling sensation. Watching outside the portholes you can clearly see things zip on by, stars, planets, nebulae, and lots of unexplained colorful weird stuff. Without any way of slowing down, really it comes by as a complete blur each time you slip.

We arrived back at where the outpost was supposed to be, right where we had pierced through the CMB radiation twice already by now. At this point you can clearly see the penetration point, it appearing less dense each time we poke through it. We went through without hesitation, and there we were. We began to call this Universe 2, or U2 for short. Again, we focused our optics and did our best to determine a good target. We had a lot of resources to keep us alive for a while longer, but they were not infinite. Our destination had to be fruitful. Then we found it.

There was a slip on this side as well! Just like the first, we found this one on accident. We started moving towards our destination when we stumbled down the slip... The sensation was the same, as if you were being tumbled around in one direction, and things blurred on by in just the same manner as our slip. When we finished however, when we arrived, it was not at all what we were hoping for or expecting. One sun, surrounded in orbit by more green and blue planets than the eyes can see. It was like the rings of Saturn, except the rings were made of planets! Upon close examination - these were Earths! There were approximately a million Earths, all slightly different, in synchronous orbit around a single star.

Gazing in awe at this incredible sight, we couldn't help but wonder how such a phenomenon could have come to be. Had there been multiple Big Bangs that created these Earths and their orbits around this sun? Or was it the result of some advanced civilization's experiment? Was this an illusion, a trick of light?

As we examined these multiple earths, we realized that it was not an illusion but a phenomenon we had never seen before. Each Earth in synchronous orbit around the same star seemed to have its own unique characteristics, each of them inhabited. We landed on one of these Earths and made contact with the inhabitants, who were surprised to see us but eager to learn more about our origins.

We explained our mission and our search for a new home, and they graciously offered to help us in any way they could. They shared their knowledge of the other Earths in and helped us devise a plan to explore them all. The inhabitants explained that their universe was formed from a singular event, a cosmic explosion that created multiple Earths in synchronous orbit around a single star. Each Earth had its own unique climate, geography, and flora and fauna. Some were lush and green, while others were barren and desolate, but they all shared certain characteristics that suggested a common origin. They were all identical in size, nearly identical in water/land ratio, and for the most part - full of humans.

Some of the Earths had advanced civilizations with technology far beyond ours, while others were still in their early stages of development. We encountered cultures that worshipped the stars and believed they held the key to their existence, as well as those who saw themselves as the only true inhabitants of their world.

The synchronous orbit of a million Earths around a single star seemed to defy the laws of gravity and celestial mechanics.

We also discovered that some of the Earths were facing catastrophic events that threatened their very survival. Natural disasters like earthquakes, volcanic eruptions, and hurricanes struck with alarming frequency, leaving entire populations displaced and struggling to rebuild. Some of the Earths had fallen prey to corrupt leaders or oppressive regimes, leading to conflict and suffering. We witnessed firsthand the devastating effects of war and violence, and it broke our hearts to see such senseless destruction.

Our initial excitement at discovering a network of synchronous Earths soon gave way to disappointment as we realized that none of the inhabitants shared our passion for space exploration. We had hoped to find a planet with similar aspirations and resources, but it seemed that we were alone in our desire to travel beyond their own solar systems - nobody cared for space exploration or travel. With the consensus that 'A million earths in stable orbit is enough', there was no drive or wish to explore beyond their planets and sun.

It was the general assumption that all of the other stars in their sky had millions of earths around them as well, so basically, *more of the same*. Why bother? You have to admit, it did make a little sense. They had everything here, plants and animals, good and bad, and in general most of the Earth planets were flourishing. When we attempted to discuss the topic of space travel, we were looked at as if we were the aliens... and I guess we were, for the first time, we were the aliens. At least they were human, anything but the Martians was quite a welcome.

We tried to convince them of the benefits of space travel, highlighting the scientific and technological advancements that could be made through exploration. But they remained skeptical, content with what they already had. It was a difficult realization to come to, and we struggled with feelings of isolation and disconnection from the rest of the universe.

As we distributed our data, the other Earths became aware of our Earth. We shared its history, its location, and of course every episode of The Simpsons. They really appreciated that. We became well known and legendary, and asked to go on tours to various planets, to speak at universities and science conventions. The thought that humans existed beyond their own solar system, and had come to visit them, was an exciting new concept to them. Fascinated by the slip, some agencies were developed to work towards space travel, and our ship was turned into a museum, filled with information about Earth's history, culture, and technology. We hosted lectures and workshops, teaching the inhabitants about the wonders of the universe and inspiring some of them to dream of one day exploring beyond their own sun.

Slowly but surely, interest in space travel began to grow. Agencies were established to work towards developing the necessary technologies, and our ship was invited to serve as a model for their own future missions. It was a small victory, but it gave us hope that someday, these Earths too might join us in our quest to explore the stars.

It was then that we unravelled the mystery of the million Earths. The reason they were so similar - was not that luck - they were the same Earth, but from different time periods! It would appear that Earth had been 'backed up' to this location at regular intervals. It seemed that these seemingly identical planets were not separate worlds at all, but rather different time periods of the same human evolution. They were each descendants of each other!

At first, it was a difficult concept to grasp. It turned out that Earth had been 'backed up' to this location at regular intervals. Each of these U2 Earths represented a different point in time for our planet. We studied the data more closely, and began to see similarities that suggested our theory was correct. We realized that each of these Earths represented a snapshot of its history, some were from the distant past, with dinosaurs roaming the land and primitive human societies struggling to survive. Others were from more recent times, with bustling cities and advanced technologies, but all were Earth. Our Earth.

Clearly someone, or something, cared about Earth and it's inhabitants. There was an Earth from various eras. Then we found it... The Zoo. The Martian Zoo. It was a backup of the Earth the martians had made. If all of the these planets were born of one big explosion, as we were told, then how would one as 'recent' as this be here? After investigating thoroughly, the leading hypothesis was that *we* had triggered the 'backup' when we exited the 'Martian' system. It was the Zoo, exactly as we had left it.

It would appear that when an 'outside' entity crosses the CMB into a 'foreign' timeline, the earth is backed up here. That would mean each of these earths are historical copies before 'alien' contact was made. Realizing this, if we wanted to find 'our' timeline Earth, it is entirely possible it was backed up here, somewhere, one of these million earths.

Over time, after searching endlessly for an Earth that was ours, out of the million around the sun, we realized it was impossible. Even if we tried to visit one new planet each day, that would be longer than we would survive, by a long shot. It was decided that we would work to preserve humanity. We went to the Zoo planet, and claimed it as ours. Upon landing, we could not believe it! Adam and Eve! They were there! When we crossed the CMB, it must have made a shadow-copy of Earth after we dropped them off. By now, they had multiplied. Old in their age, they were great, great, great, great grandparents. A small town, with dozens of households and farms, all from their doing. Adam and Eve were quite surprised to see us when we landed!

The holotape ends.

"Thank you for visiting the Lost Humanities exhibit."

"Please continue down the hallway towards the Martian exhibit."

Don't miss out!

Visit the website below and you can sign up to receive emails whenever Jason Jackson publishes a new book. There's no charge and no obligation.

https://books2read.com/r/B-A-DRTFB-GGQHD

BOOKS 2 READ

Connecting independent readers to independent writers.

Also by Jason Jackson

A Rise to Clarity
A Rise to Clarity - A Guide to Quitting Marijuana and Learning
to Live a Happy Life Without It

Standalone
Tales for Time Travelers